W9-CNN-997

Maggie steeled herself
for what lay ahead

"There has never been any mental illness in my family," she said calmly, deliberately. "I haven't received a blow to the head lately or sustained any trauma. I haven't taken any drugs. I am not insane."

"I'm glad," Christopher said earnestly. "Because I'm not either."

Maggie looked at him sharply. "But Robert didn't see you. You were practically touching him, and he didn't see you."

Christopher nodded. "The old man who used to live here couldn't see me either."

"But I can." Maggie practically whispered the words. She blinked, but he was still there: the perfectly structured face and sensuous lips, fawn-brown hair that tumbled over his forehead, broad, graceful shoulders that tapered into a spare waist....

I don't even dream this good, she thought dazedly.

Rebecca Flanders says she enjoys writing books with "something different" in them—as *Earthbound* has. This humorous but moving love story was partly inspired by *The Ghost and Mrs. Muir*, a classic film that "speaks to every woman's fantasy." In it the heroine has all the best of romance and none of the everyday inconveniences.

If she ever ran away, Rebecca says with a laugh, she'd head to Chesapeake Bay, one of the most romantic areas she's ever been. The sea coast lends itself to romance and mystery. Author of over fifty novels, this prolific writer is working on another love story with "something different" in it. This one, too, will be set by the sea.

REBECCA FLANDERS

EARTHBOUND

Harlequin Books

TORONTO • NEW YORK • LONDON
AMSTERDAM • PARIS • SYDNEY • HAMBURG
STOCKHOLM • ATHENS • TOKYO • MILAN

Published August 1990

ISBN 0-373-79002-3

Cover illustration © Kevin L. Mayes/The Image Bank

Chapter One

MAGGIE CASTLE WAS LATE. This was not unusual, but it was compounded by the fact that she had not written down the address, and she circled the neighborhood twice before she noticed Larry's gray Cadillac parked in front of a brick-enclosed mailbox. She swung in behind the Cadillac so abruptly that her brakes squealed and her front bumper nudged the back of Larry's car. She winced, not out of any fear of damage to the vehicles, but because this looked like a quiet neighborhood and the squealing of her brakes echoed like a siren. She did not want to get off on the wrong foot with people who might end up being her neighbors.

She got out of the car, slammed the door on her scarf and wasted another few minutes unlocking the door and retrieving her scarf—and her purse, which she had left on the front seat. She took a quick look around as she started up the drive.

It was autumn, and the street was lined with a sunburst of multicolored deciduous trees, orange and red and golden yellow. The houses were all brick, Colonial or Georgian style, deeply set on spacious lots. The lawns looked as though they were maintained with scissors, and there was an air of old-world elegance and permanence about the entire neighborhood that immediately struck a chord in Maggie. She could picture scholarly gentlemen in dressing gowns and slippers sitting before crackling fires in book-lined studies, maids in crisp white aprons serving sherry on silver trays and chamber music in the background.

The house she was going to see was on a cul-de-sac, at the end of Walnut Street. Set slightly higher than the others, it had an air of distinction and superiority. Its lawn, in contrast to its neighbors', was littered with leaves and weeds, and she noticed more than one loose brick in the walk. But the charm of the stately facade easily outbalanced those minor signs of neglect. *Who would ever have thought,* she mused, gazing up at the gleaming second story windows, *that I would live in a place like this?*

The front door was double-paneled natural mahogany, inset with two windows of what looked to Maggie to be Tiffany glass and decorated by a brass lion's head knocker. The brass could have used polishing, and so could the glass, but Maggie was not distracted by minor details. As Larry had told her on more than one occasion, she was a sucker for curb appeal.

She tried the door, found it locked, and began to search through her purse for the key she was certain Larry had given her in case he was late meeting her. Not that he had ever been late for anything in his life, but she did remember requesting a key just in case something came up....

She was just about to dump the contents of her purse on the porch and search through it when the door swung open. She looked at Larry defensively. "I didn't lose my key."

"Of course you didn't," he replied mildly, "because I didn't give you one. I started to, remember, and then decided you'd just lose it."

She frowned a little in annoyance, then dismissed the incident. "I'm sorry I'm late," she said, brushing his cheek with a kiss as she stepped inside. "And I bumped into your car. No damage."

"No problem. I took out extra insurance the moment I met you. And you're not late," he added a little smugly. "I told you to meet me a half hour before I planned to get here."

She spared him one brief look of exasperation and amusement. He knew her entirely too well.

But then her attention was taken by the wide marble foyer and the curving staircase before her, and she let out a breath of admiration. "Wow. Some place, huh?"

"I don't think it's what you want, but it won't hurt to have a look around, I guess. The cleanup crew didn't do a very good job. The place has been empty for almost six months, and it's going to need some work before I show it to the general public."

Maggie's heels made a satisfying clicking sound as she crossed the foyer into what appeared to be a parlor. Here the floors were hardwood, and an ugly gas heater had been set inside a small marble fireplace. The walls were painted seafoam green, with darker patches where pictures had been recently removed. But the crown molding was elaborately carved and the baseboards were five-inch mahogany.

"This color hasn't been in fashion since the fifties," Larry said with a grimace. "I guess the whole place will have to be repainted. The owners aren't going to like that."

"Who are the owners?" Maggie asked absently. The focal point of the room was a set of French doors that overlooked a tangled garden and flooded the room with a gentle light. She went over to open them.

"They live in Michigan. They were the only heirs when old man Lambrough died, which is why it took so long to get the place on the market—and why it's in such bad shape. I gather his health was failing for a long time."

"Roses!" Maggie exclaimed, stepping out onto the small patio. "And look—a fountain. Do you suppose it works?"

Larry followed her. "I doubt it. You'd have to bring a landscape architect in to get this garden in order again."

With rising excitement, Maggie went back inside and through a set of sliding double doors, where she found exactly what she expected to find: a study paneled in warm oak, lined with bookshelves and centered on a large fireplace.

"We'll have to carpet throughout," Larry commented.

"Don't be ridiculous. Why would you want to cover up these beautiful floors?"

"This place is as drafty as a barn as it is," Larry returned dismissively, "and nobody wants to take care of hardwood floors these days. It'll never sell like this."

Maggie turned around slowly, soaking in the atmosphere of age and solidity and imagining long, quiet evenings reading before the fire. An Oriental rug here, a ginger-jar lamp there, a deep, overstuffed wine leather chair...

"Somebody loved this place once," she murmured.

Larry gave her an odd look, and she explained. "Just look at all the detail. The moldings, the carving on the fireplace—did you notice the sculpture on the chandelier mount in the foyer? This is a house that was meant to be appreciated, not just lived in."

"Wait until you see the kitchen," Larry replied dryly.

Even Maggie had to admit that the kitchen was not exactly a gourmet chef's dream. It was far too large, the floor was covered in faded yellow linoleum, and someone had painted the cabinets a dull white. There wasn't enough light, and there were only three electrical outlets. But none of that bothered Maggie, who was hardly a gourmet chef and who always managed, sometimes deftly and sometimes clumsily, to avoid entertaining at home.

Looking out upon another view of the back garden was a formal dining room, which was also meaningless to Maggie except for the fact that she liked the idea of having a formal dining room. "You could always turn it into an exercise room," Larry suggested skeptically, and Maggie gave him a withering look.

Upstairs there were three bedrooms, one of which was shaded by a huge oak tree whose branches practically scraped the window. The wallpaper was a hideous dusky-rose pattern and the windows had been painted shut, but the room had a working fireplace with delicate roses and cherubs carved into the mantle. Maggie decided on the spot that would be her bedroom.

A stained-glass window filtered patterns of rose-and-yellow light over the landing, and Maggie stood at the top of the stairs for a moment, admiring it.

"I suppose I could knock out that window and put in a clear skylight," Larry speculated. "That shouldn't be too expensive, and it sure would brighten up this tomb."

"You'll do no such thing," Maggie said adamantly. "How much?"

Larry looked at her blankly.

"How much what?"

"How much for the house? You've found a buyer."

He shook his head impatiently. "Oh, come on, Maggie, you don't want this place."

Maggie tossed him a look of repressed amusement over her shoulder as she started down the stairs. "Some real-estate agent you are."

"I mean it. There's not enough closet space, the kitchen is a nightmare, and there's only one bathroom."

"So? I'm only one person. How many bathrooms do I need?"

"This place is fifty years old if it's a day. God only knows what shape the plumbing's in, not to mention the wiring. It doesn't even have air-conditioning or central heat, for Pete's sake. It'll be one headache after another. Let's have another look at that condo on the Bay."

"I don't want to live on the Bay. Too many sea gulls. And it's too far away from work."

"Okay, what about that house in Chateau Blanc? Jacuzzi, walk-in closets, recreation club. . ."

Maggie made a face. "Who wants to live in a subdivision called Chateau Blanc? Besides, I don't want a Jacuzzi."

"*Everyone* wants a Jacuzzi. It's the hottest-selling point on my list."

"I like this house. It's got character."

"It's also got dry rot and radon gas."

"Boy, if there's one thing I hate, it's a pushy salesman."

"I have your best interests at heart, honey. And believe me, this house isn't for you."

They had reached the shelf-lined room Maggie had already come to think of as the library, and she turned, raising one eyebrow eloquently. "Are you suggesting *I* don't know what's best for me?"

"Well," Larry admitted ruefully, "you aren't the most together person I've ever met."

"Just because I'm a little absentminded some-times..."

"And," he added more seriously, "you know your-self this inheritance has been eating a hole in your pocket since you got it. Sometimes when people come into money, suddenly they're a little blinded by just how much it will buy and they do, well, crazy things."

Now her expression grew impatient. "Do you see me driving a new Mercedes? Dripping in diamonds and mink coats? Come off it, Larry, I might be a little scat-terbrained now and then but I am *not* impractical. Especially when it comes to money."

"All right, I apologize."

Sometimes it irritated Maggie how easily he gave up a fight. He came forward, his hands extended and his smile at its most endearing. "I admit, in most matters you're one of the most levelheaded women I've ever known. But you're a scientist, not a real-estate broker. Take a little advice when it's offered, huh?"

Somewhat reluctantly she let him take her hands, strongly suspecting she was being patronized. Usually his playful let-me-take-care-of-you-little-girl attitude only amused her, but today she found it provoking.

Maggie was accustomed to being patronized, espe-cially by men. At five feet, three inches and one hundred two pounds she did not present a particularly imposing figure. Her short, curly dark hair and heart-shaped face only reinforced an air of vulnerability. Even with the oversize horn-rimmed glasses that she wore for reading and classroom work, she had difficulty looking older than sixteen and was often mistaken for a student at the junior college where she taught. But she was twenty-eight years old. She resented the constant struggle to get people to take her seriously and allow her to manage her own life—even when that struggle was against someone as well-meaning and good-natured as Larry.

Her voice was a little cool as she reminded him, "You're the one who told me real estate was a good investment."

"And so it is, if you know what you're doing. That's why I'm telling you this house is not for you. It will fall down around your ears before you realize one penny of what you've put into it."

For the sake of expediency, Maggie pretended to consider what he was saying. She left him and walked over to the fireplace, running her hand over the smooth finish of the wood mantle, imagining how many other hands had done the same thing, how many other voices had filled this room, how many dramas had been played out before this fireplace, right here where she stood. She knew she could not make a man like Larry understand how she felt about the sense of continuity and solidity this house exuded, but for the sake of their relationship she was compelled to try.

"The first sixteen years of my life," she said, caressing the molding along one shelf, "I lived in military housing. After the divorce, my mom and I lived in one apartment after another, and not many were better than military housing, I'll tell you that. Then there were college dorms, and now it's apartments again...."

She turned and told him simply, "I have never, ever lived somewhere I could put a nail in the wall. Every single place I've had has been just like the last one, and

For a moment she thought he wouldn't take the check. But at last he tucked it into his pocket, shaking his head. "Easiest sale I've ever made."

"Hardest *buy* I've ever made," Maggie returned, her eyes twinkling. And then, unable to contain herself a moment longer, she laughed out loud and threw her arms around him. "Oh, Larry, thanks for finding this place for me! I just know I'm going to be happy here!"

She tilted her face up to look at him, her arms still looped companionably about his neck, experiencing a surge of warmth toward him that reminded her why she had been with Larry longer than any man she had ever known. "You *are* nice," she said softly. "Sometimes I think I don't appreciate you enough."

He kissed her playfully on the lips. "Sometimes I think you're right."

A prickle of guilt caused Maggie to lower her eyes briefly. Being serious with Larry was difficult for her and not something she did often. But it occurred to her now that the least he deserved was an explanation. "Larry..."

She lifted her eyes to him again. She did not like it when people refused to look her straight in the eye when she was speaking, and she would not be guilty of the same practice, no matter how uncomfortable it made her. "I know we've been seeing each other for a long time...."

"Eighteen months," he supplied helpfully.

"And I know you expected more of a, well, commitment from me by now."

"Once you reach thirty," he told her gently, "playing the field isn't as much fun as it used to be. You start thinking about settling down."

She nodded, fighting the impulse to shift her eyes away from the tender light in his. "I just want you to know that—it's not you personally. I have trouble with long-term planning." She ventured a weak smile, toying with his lapel. "I just need some time, that's all."

He smiled at her. "Fortunately I'm a patient man."

And a soberness came into his eyes as he added, "Honey, I know how difficult it's been for you, always having to prove yourself to the world, jumping from one place to the other and never having a real home.... Commitments frighten you, and I understand that. I don't want to push you. And—" he lifted one arm to indicate their surroundings "—if buying this white elephant will make you more secure, then I'm all for it."

Maggie felt a weight lift from her shoulders, and her smile was as much one of gratitude as it was of happiness. She stroked his cheek. "I do love you, you know," she said softly. But then she felt compelled to add honestly, "I'm just not sure if it's in the way you want me to."

He kissed her gently. "Well, that's a start at least."

Then he took her hands and squeezed them lightly. "Come on, let's go back to my office and start the paperwork on this monster."

She hesitated. "Oh, Larry— I don't want to leave yet. I don't have another class this afternoon, and I'd really like to just wander around for a while, maybe do some measuring."

He glanced at his watch. "I do have another appointment in half an hour."

"Go ahead," she urged him. Suddenly she wanted more than anything in the world to be alone in her house. *Her* house. "I promise I'll lock up when I leave."

After a moment he handed her the key. "Make sure all the doors are locked," he cautioned her. "Not just the front one."

"I will."

"Okay, then. I'll let you know as soon as I get an answer from Michigan, but it might not be today."

"They'll say yes," Maggie assured him confidently.

He grinned. "From the look in your eye, they'd better."

He kissed her goodbye, and Maggie stood at the front door and waved as he drove away.

The house was eerily silent as she turned back inside, and for a moment—just a moment—she was overwhelmed by the impulsiveness of her decision. Forty-five minutes ago she had been nothing but a twenty-eight-year-old teacher, a little windblown, a little disorganized and half an hour late. Now she was a homeowner. After a moment's thought, she decided she liked that feeling.

Impetuous was not a word Maggie would generally use to describe herself. She lived her life in the comfort and security of numbers and the scientific method; she had ultimate faith in the process of logic wherein, if each step were taken carefully, precisely and in the correct order, every equation would come to a satisfying and predictable conclusion. She assured herself that what may have seemed like impulse to Larry had actually been a decision arrived at by the same carefully thought out methods by which she guided the rest of her life. Real estate was a good investment. She liked this house. She could afford this house. The tax-deductible mortgage interest was a bonus, and by taking a second mortgage to finance the renovations, she could double her savings while the value of the house appreciated. It was all very logical and reasonable. Besides, it simply *felt* right.

She walked through the house again, luxuriating in the pride of ownership. At last, here was something that belonged only to her, and more important, it was a place where *she* belonged. No more disconnecting and reconnecting utilities every year or two. No more misdirected mail. She could even have personalized stationery printed, now that she knew she wouldn't be moving before she used it up. And the next time she bought furniture, she wouldn't have to be guided by whether or not each piece would fit into the next apartment; from now on everything would have a permanent place of its own.

She didn't understand how Larry could call this place a white elephant. How could he fail to see the care that had gone into the construction, the craftsmanship in every detail? There wasn't a piece of drywall or plywood in the place, every board was hand fitted, and even after fifty years of settling, there wasn't a single crack anywhere. Houses simply weren't built like this anymore.

It was true, there wasn't much closet space, but Maggie didn't have many clothes. The bedroom would be charming redecorated in burgundy-and-pink country prints, and a coat of bold melon paint would do wonders for the downstairs parlor, setting off her rather nondescript white living-room suite to perfection. Her mind was racing with remodeling and redecorating ideas, and she chuckled softly in anticipation. She had never really had a hobby before, and bringing this old place to life was going to be *fun*.

She stood in the middle of the library, smiling to herself in contentment. "Just goes to show what you know,

Larry Hanes,'' she murmured. ''This house is going to be the best thing that ever happened to me.''

''I hate to disagree,'' said a male voice behind her, ''but I'm afraid you may want to reconsider.''

Maggie whirled and gasped as a man stepped out of the shadows.

Chapter Two

"YOUR BOYFRIEND WAS RIGHT, you know," the man went on easily, coming forward into the light. "This house will give you nothing but headaches. The place is much older than you think, and some of the plumbing is original. As for the wiring—well, it's a wonder there hasn't been a fire already. It was put in over thirty years ago, and what a mess that was."

He gave a grimace of disgust. "Holes drilled everywhere, walls torn down . . . what people will do for the sake of convenience. And then there's the matter of the heating. Even I must admit it can get quite nippy when the wind blows off the bay, and surely you aren't thinking of trying to put in a modern furnace?"

He shook his head thoughtfully. "All in all, I do think you'd do best to reconsider. I promise you don't know what you're getting into."

For a time Maggie was so taken aback she could do nothing but stare. He was one of the most striking men she had ever seen, and she was so caught up in looking at him that the significance of his words was completely lost on her. He was tall and slender, an effect that was emphasized by the black turtleneck and tight black pants he wore. His soft brown hair swept back from a high forehead, then parted naturally in the middle and tapered toward his collar, longish and somewhat shaggy in back. His eyes were deep set, dark brown, soulful and arresting. His complexion was beautifully fair, his cheekbones high, his nose aquiline and his lips perfectly etched. Maggie's first impression was that he looked like an artist, but she quickly revised that. In fact he looked like someone an artist would paint. Classic features, unforgettable beauty and the kind of understated grace and poise that very few men—or women, for that matter—could carry off well. But what was he doing in her house?

At last she recovered her breath sufficiently to demand, "Who are you? How did you get here?"

"I beg your pardon." He made a small bow from the waist. "My name is Christopher Durand. And you are—"

"M-Maggie. Maggie Castle."

"Charmed, I'm sure." He turned to run his hand lightly over the mantelpiece, just as she had done only a few minutes before. "Of course," he went on, "he was wrong about a great many other things. This house is as structurally sound as the day it was built, and it most certainly will *not* fall down around your ears." There was what might well have been a note of indignation in his tone. "It was built to last and last it will, another hundred years or more, barring earthquake, flood or—" he cast his eyes warily toward the ceiling "—electrical fire."

Abruptly, Maggie snapped out of the spell his easy manner and musical drawl had woven around her. "Excuse me," she said forcefully, "but how did you get here? What are you doing here?"

He looked down at her as though the very audacity of her statement surprised him. "My dear girl, I might well ask you the same question. After all, this is my house."

"Your—" She broke off in dismay, staring at him. "But...but I just put down a deposit. No one has even seen the house but me, and no one could have bought it without going through Larry. Unless..." A thought occurred to her, and she seized on it hopefully. "Are you one of Mr. Lambrough's heirs?"

"Hmm?" He frowned a little. "Oh, you must mean the fellow who used to live here." He walked over to the doorway, seeming to lose interest. "Odd old codger, locking himself up in here all these years by himself. I rather felt sorry for him. Look at that." He slid the double doors back and forth on their casters, pleased. "Still as smooth as silk."

"Because if you are—" Maggie followed him eagerly, hardly allowing his last words to register "—I want you to know that I really love this house. Whatever you're asking—within reason, of course," she added quickly, "I'm sure the place is worth it. If you're afraid I won't be able to keep it up, you don't have to worry. I'm well able to afford maintenance and whatever repairs it needs...."

She couldn't believe she was rattling on like this to a prospective seller; she was usually much more collected. She could practically hear the cash register ringing in his head, but she couldn't help it. She *did* want this house. She had hardly realized how much until now.

"Look, I can understand if you're reluctant to sell a home that's been in the family this long, but I promise you I'll take care of it. I understand how many memories it must hold for you, and I don't know what else to say except to assure you that I will treasure it."

He looked up from his examination of the door, turning an odd, thoughtful look on her. "I believe you will," he murmured.

She released a breath of relief. "Then it's all right? You'll let me have the house?"

"I hardly see what I can do to stop you," he replied with a negligent shrug, and went through the double door into the adjoining parlor.

Puzzled, Maggie followed him. "But I thought..."

"Lord, what a hideous color." He stood in the center of the parlor, his hands in his pockets, his expressive face forming a grimace of distaste as he looked around. "When did they do this? Of course, it's not as bad as the wallpaper upstairs, I suppose. Is it still that despicable rose pattern? I haven't checked in a while."

She nodded mutely.

"I can't imagine how anyone could sleep in a room like that. Personally, I can't understand why anyone would want to cover the walls at all. The beauty of the wood was meant to shine through, don't you agree? And I personally selected only the best...fruitwood and teak, and heart of pine for this room, so it would reflect the light."

Maggie blinked, confused. "Excuse me?"

He walked over to the mantle and inspected it appreciatively. "Ah, well, at least they didn't paint the mantle. That was all the rage for a while, too, I'm afraid. This marble was imported from Italy, you know. So was the tile in the foyer."

Maggie shook her head dumbly. "No," she managed in a moment. "I didn't know." Then she cleared her throat, becoming a little worried. "Excuse me, but just what *is* your asking price?"

He gave her another one of those odd looks, as though he suspected her of being just a bit dim-witted. "My dear, I haven't the faintest notion. This house is not mine to sell."

"But...you said it was yours! You said you were Mr. Lambrough's heir."

"I said nothing of the kind."

Her gasp of alarm was all but swallowed up in spiraling indignation. "But you...you led me to believe— Who *are* you?" she demanded furiously.

He walked over to the French doors and opened them. He stood on the threshold with his hands folded behind his back and gazed around the overgrown garden with interest. "My word," he murmured, "someone certainly has let this place go. You'll have the very devil of a time getting it back in order again, if it can be done at all."

Maggie took an angry step toward him, then thought better of it and took one small step back. If he wasn't the legal owner, he was an intruder. And though heaven knew he didn't look—or sound—dangerous, she was alone in an empty house with someone who had no right to be there. There was no point taking any chances.

She squared her shoulders and told him coolly, "You are trespassing. I suggest you leave immediately."

He turned, and she was surprised by the twinkle in his dark eyes, the slight upward tilt of his lips in private amusement. "And just where, exactly," he inquired politely, "do you suggest I go?"

Maggie was flustered, as much by the unexpected question as by the disarming and unmistakably attractive merriment in his eyes. Her gaze swept over his lean, dark-clothed figure again, the inquiring tilt of his head,

the graceful, even sexy, stance he assumed. Dangerous? Undoubtedly. But perhaps not in the strictly
physical way.

She swallowed hard and forced determination into
her voice. "I'm sure I don't care. But this is private
property and you've got no business here. If you know
what's good for you you'll get out now before you get
into real trouble."

That was an empty threat and he must have known it.
There was no telephone, and she could hardly call the
police. She was all alone here in an empty house, and
rescue, if she needed it, would probably come too late.
The sensible thing to do would have been for *her* to run,
but Maggie was not always sensible when it came to her
rights as an individual. She was the daughter of a sol-
dier and she refused to retreat without a fight.

The man came back inside, leaving the doors open to
the fresh autumn air, and crossed the room to the library. Maggie followed helplessly. "This wood is cypress, you know," he commented. "It's darkened
beautifully with age, hasn't it?"

Once again Maggie was taken aback by his abrupt
change of subject, and she found herself stammering,
"I—I thought it was oak."

He gave a brusque shake of his head, causing his
glossy brown hair to ripple attractively in the light.
"Certainly not. An ordinary builder would have used
oak. Cypress is much more durable, especially in this
climate. It doesn't crack, you see, or swell with mois-
ture or heat, and one must be particularly careful when
designing shelves. You don't want them to warp. Of
course," he added matter-of-factly, "I doubt anyone
would think of using cypress today. It was much easier
to come by when this house was built."

Something within Maggie was cautiously intrigued. True, he was an intruder, and he was beginning to make her very uncomfortable. But he hardly seemed inclined toward violence, and he *did* seem to know a great deal about the house. Or had he merely guessed that the quickest way to win her confidence was to center the conversation on her new and greatest weakness, her house?

Watching him warily for unexpected moves, she said, "Larry said the house was over fifty years old."

"A great deal over," he agreed. "The final nail was driven in 1895."

"Nonsense," Maggie replied immediately. "This neighborhood isn't nearly that old."

"Of course not." He made a gesture toward the window. "All these other houses grew up around it much later. Of course, I am flattered to notice they imitated my style, but it is rather a shame they crowded out the view. It used to be quite spectacular, nothing but meadows and forest as far as the eye could see. As much thought should go into designing the view as into the construction of the house itself, and I knew the moment I saw it this property was unsurpassed. This house was a country retreat within shouting distance of town."

A prickle of uneasiness started at the base of Maggie's spine, one she could not precisely explain. She had been so busy worrying about who he was and what he intended to do that she had not been paying strict attention to what he said. Something about those last few sentences, however, jangled her attention into sharpened alertness. A common burglar? Hardly. With that cultured accent and educated, even courtly way of speaking, he would have been more at home in a European museum than in an abandoned house in Chesapeake Bay, Maryland. He couldn't be over thirty years old, yet he spoke as though he had made his life's work studying this house and its environs. A country retreat? Since when could the suburbs of Baltimore be considered a country retreat?

She inquired cautiously, "How do you know all this?"

His smile was kind and slightly condescending. "I'm sure I told you. This is my house."

"You mean you used to live here."

"I mean I built it," he replied patiently and without a flicker of humor.

"You told me," Maggie replied cautiously, "that the house was built in 1895."

"Precisely."

Maggie felt a tightening of her chest muscles. Worse than a burglar; he was a nut. And she was trapped in here with him.

She tried, with all her might, to remain calm. She even managed a rather vague, somewhat patronizing smile. "And just how old are you?"

His dark, artfully sculpted brows came together thoughtfully. "I'm not precisely sure. What year is it?"

Maggie released a slow, shaky breath. *Weird,* she thought. *Definitely weird.* The smartest thing she could do was run for the door, but what if her flight startled him into violence? His stride was undoubtedly longer than hers, and she had already seen him move with the grace of a cat; he could overtake her in seconds. She had absolutely no experience whatsoever with psychopaths, and all she could think to do was to stay calm and keep him talking. Meanwhile, her eyes began to scan the room circumspectly for a weapon.

When she didn't answer immediately, he shrugged his shoulders and said, "Ah, well, it doesn't matter. I am at least twenty-five or thirty years older than this house."

Maggie found her voice. "You're remarkably well preserved," she returned politely.

"Thank you," he replied. His eyes twinkled again as he tucked his hands into the pockets of his slacks. "Of course, I can't really take any credit for that. It's one of the benefits of my condition."

"Your...condition?"

Upon the hearth, half hidden in the shadows of the fireplace, was an iron poker, and Maggie's heart gave a lurch. As unobtrusively as possible, she began to edge toward it.

"Indeed, my condition." He cleared his throat, either in genuine or feigned discomfiture, and confessed, "Although I find this somewhat awkward, it's clear you haven't deduced the truth. The fact of the matter is that I am, well, deceased."

Maggie stopped where she was and stared at him. This was worse than she thought. It was obvious he had far more imagination than the average psychopath. The situation was growing more dire by the moment.

She murmured, because she simply couldn't think of anything else to say, "I'm sorry to hear that."

"You're sorry? You should take it from my point of view."

He looked at her then, as though seeing her for the first time. His gaze moved thoughtfully from the top of her curls to the tips of her ankle boots, taking in every detail from her small, gold ball earrings to the short wool jacket, and long dirndl skirt and the seven-foot-long cotton scarf draped around her neck. Maggie found being the recipient of such a studied examination uncomfortable, to say the least, and was relieved when he said, "Interesting."

He returned his gaze to her face, and his smile was easy and relaxed, without a hint of malice. "In fact, you are an interesting young woman. I believe I like you."

"I'm so glad," Maggie said weakly.

His smile deepened, and his eyes took on a gleam of conspiratorial amusement. "Of course, you realize that the average person would have put it all together much sooner, but I don't hold that against you. I've never been particularly impressed with the average."

Maggie took another hesitant, shuffling step toward the fireplace. He didn't stop her, nor did he seem to even notice. "And you don't appear to be in the least bit frightened," he went on. "The average person would be."

"Why should I be frightened?" Maggie replied evenly. "You're not going to hurt me, are you?"

"Certainly not." He seemed insulted by the suggestion. "It's simply that most people wouldn't react to an encounter with a discarnate being quite so equitably."

"Well, you've already said that I'm not like most people," Maggie replied soothingly. "And I can hardly be frightened by something I don't believe in, can I?"

He appeared puzzled. "What don't you believe in?"

"Ghosts," she replied unwaveringly. She was close enough to the fireplace to feel confident now. One swift grab and the poker would be hers.

He made a face. "That's such a pedestrian term."

"It doesn't matter what you call them. I don't believe in them."

He seemed to be amused. "Well, under the circumstances I would say it hardly matters whether you believe or not." He patted his chest and his abdomen; he looked down at his feet and stretched out his arms. "I am unmistakably here."

"But that doesn't mean you're a ghost."

"I've just told you I am."

Maggie cast a brief glance toward the poker and hoped he didn't notice. Even if he did, he was on the other side of the room and couldn't possibly reach the weapon before she did. "Then prove it," she challenged him, her gaze steady.

"How?"

"Do something ghostly. Disappear or walk through a wall or rattle chains or something."

"Parlor tricks," he scoffed, "are for children."

Maggie lunged for the fireplace and came up with the poker firmly gripped in both hands, poised near her shoulder like a baseball bat. "All right," she told him, breathing hard. "I don't want to hurt you."

He appeared neither surprised nor concerned. "Don't worry. You couldn't possibly."

She began to back cautiously toward the door. Her heart was pounding with adrenaline, and her words were a little choppy. "I'm leaving now. Just stay away from me and everything will be all right. Don't try to stop me."

"I wish you wouldn't go. I'd like to talk to you some more."

The ten feet that stretched between Maggie and the door suddenly seemed unbearable. Giving in to a rush of panic, she turned and fled.

Suddenly, impossibly, he was standing in front of the door. Two seconds ago he had been on the other side of the room; now he was standing not four feet in front of her, solidly blocking her way. She hadn't even seen him move.

A blinding pulse of primal fear exploded, ancient survival instincts took over, and with a cry Maggie threw the poker with all her might. At that distance there was no way she could miss him; at that distance the blow would probably knock him unconscious, if not worse. Maggie knew all that in a rush of horror and regret only a split second before she saw the poker pass through his body, bounce against the wall and clatter harmlessly to the floor.

The scene replayed in slow motion in her mind once, twice and a third time. The heavy iron poker flying through the air, meeting his form at the shoulder unimpeded and passing through him as though he were nothing more than a holographic image. She saw again the way he arched his eyebrow, as though in disapproval of her display, and the way he turned to pick up the poker and offer it politely to her.

And then Maggie was running. Somehow she managed to squeeze past him, somehow she jerked open the front door, somehow she unlocked her car and started the engine. And the next thing she remembered she was sitting in the parking lot of a convenience store some ten blocks away, gripping the steering wheel and shaking convulsively.

She did not know how long she sat there, watching the traffic speed by on the street in front of her, trembling and trying to breathe deeply. At last her head began to clear, and the only thing she could think of was that she was lucky to be alive—not because of what had just happened in the house, but because she was obviously in no condition to be behind the wheel of a car.

After a while she turned off the engine and loosened her seat belt. She ran her fingers through her hair, and her hand came away damp with perspiration. She leaned her head back against the headrest and took a deep breath, releasing it slowly through pursed lips. "Okay," she muttered softly to herself. "It's all over. You're okay."

But she wasn't okay. How could she be okay when she had just seen the impossible with her own eyes? What had just happened to her in that house defied logic, defied reason, and the only possible conclusion she could draw was that she was having a breakdown, losing her mind.... But she couldn't afford to have a breakdown. She refused to have a breakdown! She was a scientist, and things like this shouldn't happen to her. *God, don't let this be happening to me....*

She clenched her hands on the steering wheel and closed her eyes tightly against the rising hysteria. The whooshing sound of passing traffic was reassuring. The bright autumn sun, magnified through the windshield, was hot on her face and it felt good. Slowly she opened her eyes and concentrated fiercely on the sights and sounds of ordinary life around her. She watched people coming and going from the convenience store for a time. A family of four in a car with Ohio license plates pulled up to the gas pumps, and Maggie speculated idly about what kind of trip they were on. After a while she felt calmer. Almost rational. And she could look back on what had happened to her at the house with some measure of detachment.

She was not having a breakdown. It was very simple, really. She hadn't really seen a fireplace poker fly through a man's body as though he were made of air. She was certain of that. She had been scared; she had been running. How could she be sure what she had seen? And all that crazy talk about ghosts ... it was no wonder her mind had started playing tricks on her. Hysteria, that was all it had been. And although Maggie had never been hysterical in her life, nor even considered herself prone to the symptoms, that was as good an explanation as any.

There was a pay phone a few dozen yards in front of her, and she knew she should get out and call the police. But there wasn't a chance in a thousand that the intruder would still be around, and the police could hardly do anything now. It wasn't as though she was reporting an attempted rape or assault, and there wasn't anything in the house for him to steal. Of course, he had been trespassing, and it was her civic duty to report a crazy person wandering loose in the neighborhood, but she wasn't up to dealing with the police just yet. She would go home, have a glass of wine and then call the police.

It would be an exaggeration to say that Maggie was able to put the incident out of her mind. But by the time she stopped by the grocery store, stood in line at the checkout counter and maneuvered her way through the late-afternoon traffic to her apartment building, she was able to put the matter in perspective. That was the secret to a balanced life, Maggie firmly believed: simply putting things in their proper perspective.

She had been raised in what her father called the military way of thinking: concise, concrete and ordered. There were rules for everything; patterns even in chaos. If one followed those rules and searched for those patterns, the ultimate reward would be order, and with order came control. It didn't matter whether the problem was in quantum physics, military strategy or choosing what to wear for a date, the same methods applied. And although Maggie occasionally had some difficulty creating order out of the chaos of her personal life, she had ultimate faith in the powers of clear thinking. All that was required was that she establish priorities and determine the appropriate response to the situation.

The physical laws of matter did not allow for the displacement of mass by a fireplace poker without visible damage to said mass. There had never been any clinical evidence to prove the existence of ghosts. There was therefore only one explanation: that what she thought she had seen had been a momentary aberration, a trick of the eye or even a bit of sleight of hand on the part of the stranger. It had happened, but not the way she'd perceived it. Very simple, really, and nothing to worry about at all.

She was almost certain of it.

Once she had exhausted intellect, Maggie allowed herself the privilege of some purely emotional responses. The first was a very appropriate and healthy sense of indignation. How dare that man break into her house and pretend to be the owner? How dare he draw her in with all that talk about cypress shelves and imported marble and then—*then*—calmly announce that he was dead? What a fool he must have thought her. And indeed she had been a fool for not leaving the house and calling the police the minute she spotted him.

Resentment followed on the heels of indignation, because he had ruined her first afternoon alone in the only house she had ever owned. It should have been a special time for her, but he had robbed her of the pleasure. Maggie didn't believe in omens any more than she believed in ghosts, but she couldn't help suspecting that she would replay this unpleasant episode in her head every time she entered the house from now on. His intrusion into her personal time was like a blemish on a perfect piece of fruit, and it wasn't fair.

Not that he had at all changed her mind about the house. If that had, in some twisted way, been his intention, he was to be sorely disappointed. Once Maggie Castle made up her mind, it stayed made up, and she had never felt as strongly about anything as she did about buying that house. No sexy-looking, smooth-talking, half-crazed cat burglar was going to frighten her away. If she had to put bars on the windows and double locks on all the doors, she would. But that house was *hers*.

As the drama of the experience faded into the background, taking with it some of the worst of her anger and all of her shock, Maggie had to admit to a very definite sense of curiosity. Who *was* he, and what had brought him to her house, of all the houses on the street? Had he followed her in, or worse, had he been lurking about in the shadows for hours, perhaps days, just waiting for someone to come along?

She wondered if anything he had said about the house had any basis in fact. Eighteen ninety-five? She doubted it. She didn't think there were any houses that age still standing in the area, but then, what did she know? And wouldn't it be something if it were true? She could end up owning a historic landmark.

She decided to ask Larry to look into it, and that brought up another problem—whether or not to tell Larry what had happened after he left. Almost immediately she decided not to. A woman in distress would only bring out his macho protective instincts, and Maggie practically groaned out loud at the thought. He hadn't wanted her to buy the house in the first place, and there was no point in adding an unsafe neighborhood to his list of reasons. All in all, she would save herself a great many problems by just keeping quiet.

She pulled her car into the parking space in front of her neat white Colonial apartment building—a carbon copy of six other buildings in the complex, which were in turn copies of at least three other complexes in the surrounding area. But today she did not feel as depressed by the sight of her undistinguished dwelling as she usually did. Perhaps it was because she knew she would be leaving soon. Perhaps it was because, after the events of the afternoon, she was beginning to appreciate the benefits of the ordinary. The plain white building was reassuring, familiar and unsurprising. No ghosts—real, imagined or only pretending—would ever be found there. Besides, the complex was patrolled by security guards.

She took her groceries from the back of the car and carried them up the short flight of stairs to her apartment, juggling purse and grocery bag as she struggled to get the key in the lock. She wondered if Larry had tried to call yet about the contract and if she had remembered to leave her answering machine on. She suppressed a groan as she thought about the call she had yet to make to the police.

She got the door open, kicked it closed behind her and fumbled for the light switch. A tall, lanky figure rose from the sofa as the room sprang into light.

"Hello again," said Christopher Durand.

Chapter Three

THE BAG OF GROCERIES crashed to the floor, and Maggie stifled a cry. "You! How did you— What are you—"

He held up a skeleton key dangling from a small chain. She recognized it as the key Larry had given her to the house. "You forgot to lock the doors," he said.

"How did you get in here?" she croaked hoarsely.

But it didn't matter. This was too much. A blinding surge of outrage overwhelmed whatever fear the sight of him might have generated, and she turned toward the telephone in the kitchen, tripping over scattered oranges and a bag of celery. "All right, mister, this time you've gone too far. I'm calling the police!"

"That should be interesting." He dropped the key onto an end table and deftly made his way through the litter of groceries toward her. "What will you tell them?"

"Stay away from me!" Maggie shouted. She leaned over the counter and snatched the wall phone off the hook, frantically punching out three numbers.

"I only meant to point out," Christopher said mildly, picking up an orange and placing it neatly on the counter, "that once the police get here, I'm not at all sure they will be able to see me. And then what will you tell them?"

A busy signal buzzed in her ear and Maggie swore out loud. She slammed her hand against the disconnect hook and tried again. "It's not going to work this time," she informed him darkly, breathing hard, "so you can just save your breath on all that ghost garbage. I don't know how you got in here, but this complex is patrolled by security guards. I can guarantee you're not going to get out, so don't even *think* about trying to leave. We're going to get to the bottom of this once and for all!"

He seemed genuinely puzzled as he arranged his long frame on one of the bar stools at the counter. "Why should I want to leave? I just got here."

"Hello!" Maggie shouted into the phone. And then she pulled the receiver away from her ear and stared at it incredulously. "Hold!" she exclaimed. "They put me on hold!"

Christopher swiveled back and forth on the bar stool and seemed delighted with the effect. "What a comfortable set of rooms you have here," he declared warmly. His bright, busy eyes moved back over the living area, admiring the long white sofa and matching club chairs, the floor lamps with their sleek modern shades, the pastel-print cushions scattered about. "Functional yet eye pleasing. What is this carpet made of? Is that a television?"

"Answer the damn phone," Maggie muttered, keeping a wary eye on her unwanted guest as he sprang down from the stool and went to examine the television. "I could be dying here...."

But the urgency she exhibited seemed rather unnecessary, as the strange man in black displayed absolutely no interest in harming her—or in getting away. Instead, he seemed fascinated by her nineteen-inch color television set, inspecting it from one angle and then another, twisting and turning knobs to no avail.

"It doesn't appear to be operating," he announced, standing back with a studious frown.

"Keep your hands off that!"

The buzz of the front door startled Maggie so badly that she almost dropped the phone. Christopher turned his head toward the sound inquisitively, and Maggie hung up the phone and rushed toward the door. The police, at least fifteen minutes away if and when they decided to answer their phone, were of no use to her at all when there was help—or at least a witness—right at her front door.

"Stay where you are!" Maggie warned, and flung open the door.

"Hi, Ms Castle. I'm on time for a change."

It was Robert, one of the students she tutored. Of course, Maggie had forgotten they had a lesson today, and for a moment the sight of him meant absolutely nothing to her. But it didn't matter who he was or why he was here; she grabbed his arm gratefully.

"Robert, come in." She pulled him inside, casting a harried glance over her shoulder. The man in black still stood near the television, watching her with interest and no sign of concern. "I'm afraid I'm having a little trouble right now, but it's nothing I can't handle if you'll just give me a hand—"

"Sure, Ms Castle, no problem." Robert bent and began to pick up the groceries that were scattered at his feet.

"No, that's not what I meant—"

"Perhaps," suggested Christopher with only a small frown of concern on his face, "you'd better introduce us."

It was perhaps a testament to the state of Maggie's rattled mind that the suggestion seemed perfectly reasonable to her. At least she would have the man's name, which by now she had completely forgotten, and a witness to confirm it.

"Robert," she said quickly, "Forget the groceries. I'd like you to meet Mr...." She paused inquiringly.

"Durand," Christopher supplied obligingly, and stepped forward. "Christopher Durand."

"Christopher Durand," Maggie repeated triumphantly.

Robert straightened up slowly, glancing around the room, then looked at her again in respectful confusion. "Oh, yeah?"

An awful cold feeling began to tighten around Maggie's stomach. Half-believed possibilities and impossibilities were pounding at her, and the thin voice of reason whined like a siren in the back of her mind, *Be careful....*

But not yet. She was not ready to give in to madness yet.

She took Robert's shoulders and turned him deliberately so that he was facing Christopher, not eight feet away. "Robert," she said, trying hard to keep the desperation out of her voice, "look straight ahead. Over there by the television set. What do you see?"

Robert concentrated for a moment. He was looking straight at Christopher. He couldn't possibly miss him.

He glanced back at Maggie. "A magazine stand?"

Maggie's heart gave a thump and then was still. Christopher was standing in front of the magazine stand. Robert should not have even been able to *see* the magazine stand.

"Just as I suspected," Christopher said sadly, coming forward. "He can't see or hear me."

Christopher stood directly in front of Robert, waving his hand back and forth in front of the boy's eyes. Robert didn't blink. He simply stood there looking at Maggie with a cautious, very confused expression on his face. Christopher clapped his hands very loudly two inches from Robert's left ear. The sound made Maggie flinch, but Robert only said, "Ms Castle, are you all right?"

Maggie couldn't answer. Her throat felt gummy and tight, and she couldn't draw a breath. She stared at Christopher, who was as real and solid and three-dimensional to her as Robert was. *But Robert didn't see him.*

Christopher gave a sympathetic shrug of his shoulders. "This must be embarrassing for you."

"Ms Castle?" Robert's voice was edged with alarm. "You're not sick, are you? Are you going to faint? You want me to call somebody?"

Maggie's senses returned with a snap. Her mouth seemed to operate with a will of its own, spilling out words—hopefully the right words—without her even having to think about them. "No, Robert, I'm fine. I'm afraid I'm not prepared for our lesson today. Thank you for coming by. I'll call to reschedule—"

She had his arm and was leading him to the door when he said in protest, "But what about that guy you wanted me to meet?"

"Yes, of course, Mr. Christopher Durand, a very prominent person in his field. I think he could help you a lot in your studies. I want you to meet him someday, when we have more time—"

"That might prove to be difficult," murmured Christopher.

"Thanks for stopping by, Robert." Maggie shoved him out the door. "I'll call you."

Silence rang when he was gone. Maggie leaned against the door and closed her eyes, hoping that when she opened them again the room would be empty, everything would be back to normal and she would discover she had only been dreaming for the past hour or so.

She was not dreaming. She could feel the cool panel of the door against her sweaty palms, she could hear the hum of the refrigerator and smell the lingering odor of the fish she had cooked for last night's dinner. A car door slammed outside, and someone laughed in the hallway. This was very real.

She felt dizzy and disoriented, and when her chest began to hurt she realized she hadn't taken a breath in some time. Shakily she drew in air, but she did not open her eyes. She had to think. She had to *think*.

There was a man standing in her living room whom no one could see but herself. A man who defied the laws of physics when she threw a fireplace poker at him, who said he remembered life in 1895, who entered her apartment without a key. A man who claimed to be dead.

The possibilities ticked off in her head. A practical joke? Who did she know who was capable of such elaborate trickery and for what reason? And a practical joke could not explain what she had seen with her own eyes when the fireplace poker passed through Christopher Durand's less-than-solid body.

A holographic image? Great strides had been made in laser imagery recently, but the amount of bulky equipment involved, not to mention the expense, made that solution unlikely. Besides, it would not explain

Robert's lack of reaction when Christopher had waved a hand back and forth directly before his eyes. And how could a holographic image pick up an orange and place it on a counter?

But how could a ghost?

Was she under the influence of some kind of drug? A hypnotic trance? Was she at this very minute lying in a hospital bed with tubes in her arms and monitors strapped to her chest, hallucinating this entire sequence?

Was she going insane?

The shrilling of the telephone caused Maggie to jump. For two more rings she stared at the object on the wall as though she had never seen it before. Then Christopher moved toward the telephone curiously, and Maggie propelled herself toward it, snatching it off the hook with a breathless, "Hello!"

"Goodness! You sound winded. You weren't in the shower, were you?"

It took Maggie a moment to recognize her friend Elena. Christopher came around the counter and examined the design of the telephone closely; Maggie backed up and stumbled over an orange. Christopher commented, "Some improvements in design since the first model. I like it. More compact and attractive. Does it come in any other color besides yellow?"

Maggie managed to focus her attention on the voice on the other end of the telephone. "I—uh, no. I just dropped some things and was picking them up...."

"Well, leave them where they fell and meet me at Ming Lei's. It's been weeks since we had dinner together, and I'm going into Chinese-food withdrawal."

Christopher, losing interest in the telephone, began opening kitchen cabinets. Maggie twisted around to follow his movements, trying to concentrate on what Elena had said. "Dinner? Tonight? I don't think so..."

Christopher slammed one of the cabinet doors and Maggie winced. He looked at her apologetically. "Tight hinge," he observed.

"Excuse me?" said Elena's voice in her ear. "Did I just hear Maggie Castle turn down a Chinese dinner? What's the matter, are you sick?"

Christopher left the cabinets and went over to the blender. Frantically, Maggie covered the mouthpiece of the telephone with her hand. "Don't touch that!" she hissed.

"Maggie?"

Christopher looked offended but moved away from the blender. Maggie said to Elena, "No, I'm fine, really...."

"Well, then, how about if I bring over some take-out?"

"No!" Maggie practically shouted the word. Christopher came back over to her and lifted himself onto the counter, watching her with interest. Maggie took a breath and repeated in what she hoped was a calmer tone, "No, I really can't tonight. The house is a mess and I've got papers to grade and...and...Robert, yes that's it, this is his tutoring night, so you see I really can't—"

Elena's voice sounded concerned. "Maggie, are you okay? You sound really strange."

"Yes, I'm fine, really—"

"Well, I've said it before and I'll say it again: You don't get out enough. Why don't you just relax every once in a while and do something besides work? That's how mad scientists get to be mad, you know—too much time in the laboratory. First thing you know you'll be bumping into walls and hearing voices.''

Christopher cocked his head at her, and Maggie restrained an hysterical urge to laugh. If only Elena knew....

And because she didn't know how much longer she could keep up this conversation without starting to babble, Maggie said somewhat frantically, "Listen, I've got to go. I think someone's at the door."

"You're sure you don't want me to come over later?"

"Yes, yes, I'm sure. Another time, okay?" And she was already moving to hang up the phone.

"Well, all right. But stop by the shop sometime next week, okay? I'm expecting a new shipment."

"Yes, I will," Maggie promised quickly. "Goodbye."

She hung up the phone and took a deep breath, needing a moment to resolve the world of the extraordinary with the very ordinary phone call from Elena. But somehow things seemed clearer now, easier to accept. Christopher was still sitting on the counter a few feet away from her, his hands linked loosely between his knees, his expression alert but his eyes sympathetic. And as Maggie looked at him, she felt the lingering hysteria fade away.

"There has never been any mental illness in my family," she said calmly, deliberately. "I haven't received a blow to the head lately or sustained any kind of trauma. I haven't taken any drugs. I'm not under any particular stress. I am not insane."

"I'm glad," Christopher said earnestly. "Because I'm not, either."

Maggie looked at him sharply. "Robert didn't see you." Her tone rose with a note of what was almost accusation. "You were practically touching him, and he didn't see you."

Christopher nodded in agreement. "The old man who used to live in the house couldn't see me, either."

"But I can." Maggie practically whispered the words. She stared at him so long that her vision blurred; when she blinked, he was still there: that beautiful, perfectly structured face and those sensuous lips; fawn-brown hair that tumbled down slightly over his forehead and gleamed in the lamplight; long slender fingers and taut thighs; graceful dancer's shoulders that tapered into a spare waist... *I don't even dream this good,* she thought dazedly.

Impulsively she stepped forward and reached out her hand as though to touch him. He watched her curiously but made no move to flinch away. And suddenly Maggie had a vision of her hand passing through flesh and bone, of his form wavering and dissolving beneath her touch. A rush of queasiness made her shudder. She jerked her hand back and swallowed hard. She wasn't ready for that. Not yet.

She shook her head a little to clear it, her mind suddenly racing with questions. She felt as she did when she was in the midst of exploring a theorem: not fully convinced until the final line was drawn, but excited with the process of discovery, immersed in the possibilities that were offered and tantalized by the challenge.

"Then why me?" she demanded of him. "Why can I see you when no one else can?"

"I've wondered the same thing myself," Christopher admitted with a shrug. "Not that I'm complaining, mind you. It grows awfully dull, conversing with oneself. And I must say—" he gave her a disarming grin that was even more unsettling when she remembered it came from a disembodied spirit "—I do appear to have extraordinary taste when it comes to choosing my earthly companions."

Maggie smoothed her palms on her skirt and tried not to let that all-too-human twinkle in his eye distract her. "Do you mean to tell me that in all the years you've been . . . a ghost . . . no one else has ever seen you?"

"That's right."

She wanted to linger on that, to examine and dissect it until she found the reason why she, of four billion people on earth, should have been chosen for this special visitation. But too many other questions were spinning and leaping in her head, demanding equal attention.

"But. . .if you're a ghost, what are you doing here in my apartment? You should be in your house. Ghosts are supposed to haunt houses, not apartments!"

He sprang lightly down from the counter, appearing to lose interest in the conversation. "You don't say."

"Why are you here?"

"I told you, I wanted to talk to you some more." He walked over to the sink, practiced turning the water on and off, went over to the built-in oven and opened the door. "Very clever," he declared approvingly. "Compact, yet efficient. Is it brick-lined?"

"I don't know," replied Maggie impatiently. "How did you get here?"

"I'm not sure." He noticed the microwave oven and glanced at her. "Another television?"

"How do you know about television?"

"The old man used to have one. It was very stimulating for a few years, but after a while all the programs were the same."

"How did you get here?" she insisted.

He smiled at her. "I'm not sure. Perhaps you thought me here."

He left Maggie to muse over that peculiar possibility while he continued his exploration of the kitchen. Finding the dishwasher, he tugged experimentally at the door and sprang back when it swung open. "Great Scott," he exclaimed softly, "whatever can this be for?"

"It's an automatic dishwasher," she replied distract-edly.

"You don't mean it." He pulled out the bottom rack, and then the top one, examining both closely. "A washing machine for dishes? Why, next you'll be tell-ing me of food that prepares itself!"

Maggie thought of frozen dinners and microwave cakes, but didn't know how to begin to explain those to him. All the questions she was burning to ask were temporarily put aside for the fascination of watching him discover the twentieth century. *This must be real,* she thought somewhat dazedly. *It's too bizarre to be imaginary.*

Christopher pushed the racks back in place and closed the door. "But what do the servants do?"

"I don't have any servants."

He looked around the apartment with patent disbe-lief. "All this luxury, and you can't afford servants?"

"I don't need them," Maggie explained. "Hardly anyone does, anymore."

His eyes lit up with sudden understanding. "Ah," he exclaimed in soft delight. "I predicted it would come to this when the sewing machine became affordable. The drudgery of a woman's work has been completely eliminated. How perfectly marvelous. And what do you do with yourself all day, with no housework to keep you occupied?''

A tickle of hysterical amusement formed in the back of Maggie's throat and she tried not to give in to it. This was no joke. This was a very serious and challenging situation, and it was mandatory that she remain intellectually focused. But the charm of his naïveté was impossible to resist, and she found herself drawn into the unconventional interchange.

"I have a job," she informed him.

He nodded thoughtfully. "Of course. And what kind of work do you do?"

"I teach math at a junior college while I'm working on my doctoral degree in physics."

He seemed amazed. "You can't mean it! Universities are offering degrees to females now? And in physics? How extraordinary!"

His enthusiasm was entrancing, very nearly contagious, as he swept his arm about the room. "And this place—you live here alone? You come and go as you please?"

Maggie's eyes danced with repressed mirth. "Of course."

"Incredible! What a marvelous time to be a woman—or a man, for that matter. I always envisioned something of the sort, but I never thought it would be quite like this."

Suddenly Maggie was rocked by that feeling of disorientation again. Of being trapped out of time and place, overwhelmed by the swiftness with which everything she had ever considered normal was being displaced. Was she actually having a conversation with a man from the nineteenth century? Could she be hearing with her own ears the rich timbre of his voice, the cultured upper-class accent, the vibrancy of expression? Could she actually be seeing the quick, graceful movements, the lively mobility in his face, the gleam of enthusiasm in his eyes? How could this be happening to her?

She touched her head with her fingertips as though to focus concentration. "This is all happening too fast," she murmured.

He looked up curiously from his inspection of the refrigerator. "What is?"

Maggie took a breath. "You realize, of course, that there are no such things as ghosts."

"Correction," he pointed out. "There has never been any clinical evidence to prove the existence of ghosts."

She found it annoying that his thought processes seemed to be clearer than hers. "That's what I meant, of course."

"Until now."

"I think that's still open for debate."

He shrugged. "I am here. I occupy space—"

"You appear to," she corrected.

"I have mass, I interact with my environment—"

"Again, apparently."

He gave her a smile that was both indulgent and breathtakingly sweet. "Then shall we agree to say that I *appear* to exist?"

Maggie could have stamped her foot with frustration. "I don't know *what* to say!" She made a half turn, as though in search for answers, thrusting her curls back with both hands. And abruptly, she turned back to him. "What would you do if you were in my place?"

He regarded her thoughtfully for a moment. "I believe," he decided, "I would pick up my groceries from the floor and put them away."

Maggie laughed. She couldn't help it; at that moment laughter seemed the only logical, indeed, the only sane, reaction. Simple and unstrained, it bubbled forth from within her without a hint of hysteria, freeing her, however briefly, from the monumental struggle to hold on to reason. And her laughter sparked a reciprocal light in Christopher's eyes. He smiled at her, and they shared the moment like two ordinary people standing in a very ordinary kitchen in the fading light of the afternoon.

Eventually, letting the warmth of the moment linger, Maggie turned and began gathering up the groceries. Christopher knelt beside her to help.

"How do you do that?" Maggie demanded suddenly, watching him drop a bag of pasta back into the crumpled grocery sack. "You don't have a physical form. How can you manipulate physical objects?"

His eyes met hers, bright with interest. "Now that *is* a good question," he agreed.

He stretched out his hand, examining it minutely—a hand that was so close, Maggie could have shifted half an inch and brushed it with her shoulder. But she didn't dare. He reached down and picked up a can of tomato juice, slowly and with exaggerated care. He dropped it into the bag. "Fascinating," he murmured.

"Only energy can act upon matter with observable results," he pointed out. "Therefore, I must be—that is, my present form must be—some sort of energy pattern."

Maggie sat back on her heels, intrigued. "Perhaps at a slightly different vibrational level than we know on the physical plane."

"Precisely," he agreed thoughtfully. And then he smiled. "We think alike, you and I. That's refreshing."

Maggie realized with a start it was true. And it *was* refreshing to meet someone whose logic was as straightforward as her own, even if that person did happen to be slightly less than real.

"And energy can be measured," he went on. "If I can be measured, I must, indeed, exist."

Maggie's stifled giggle was a mixture of delight and disbelief. "You were worried?"

"You must admit," he replied with a twinkle in his eye, "your arguments are sound. I was beginning to wonder whether I might be only a figment of my own imagination."

She sobered slightly. "Different vibrational levels, other planes—it's all science fiction, you know."

"So is all science until it's proven fact."

She looked at him curiously as he began to scoop the remainder of the groceries into the bag. "You sound knowledgeable in the field. Of science, I mean, not science fiction. Were you a scientist?"

"Of a sort. I invented things. Unfortunately, most of my concepts were far too advanced even for that enlightened age, so I received little recognition for my efforts. I was, in fact," he confessed without a trace of shame, "a genius."

"Indeed." Maggie tried to hide her skepticism behind the filled bag of groceries as she stood and lifted it to the counter.

"Fortunately I received a bit more acclaim for my building designs. I was, for a while, quite sought after in Europe, especially Germany. The Germans have a true appreciation for the beauty inherent in simplicity and structural solidity. I once designed a home around a tree—a giant oak, as I recall, of indeterminate age. Its lower branches provided the support for the entire structure."

"A tree?" Maggie did not bother to conceal her doubt this time.

"I admit, it was a bit eccentric. But so was the gentleman who commissioned it—a baron of some sort, I believe. Most of my buildings were much more conventional."

"My house," Maggie said. "You really did build it?"

"My house," he corrected. "It was my finest accomplishment—not because it was spectacular or even unusual in any way, but because it was so perfectly suited to the needs of the owner... myself. It was a comfortable home."

"Yes," agreed Maggie softly. "That's exactly what I thought when I first saw it."

"It was one of the first in this area to have indoor plumbing incorporated into the design," he added. "And electric lamps at the top and bottom of the stairs. I generated my own electricity from a waterwheel in back of the house. I doubt if it's still there. In fact, I'm not certain the stream is even still there. But it was a great convenience not to have to carry lanterns up and down the stairs at night."

"I can imagine," Maggie murmured, once again fighting that slightly dazed sensation. She turned her attention to putting the groceries away, busying her hands to give her mind a chance to focus.

"When were you born?" she asked.

"I'm not sure." He had wandered away and was examining her stereo. "What is this?"

Maggie glanced over her shoulder. "A stereo system."

"What does it do?"

"How can you not know when you were born?"

"It was a long time ago." He lifted the glass top and examined the turntable. "Is this like a gramophone? And these boxes on the sides, are they power units?"

"They're speakers." Impatiently she turned around and braced her palms on the counter. "Listen, I've answered all your questions. The least you could do is answer a few of mine."

He appeared abashed as he looked up. "You're right, of course. I keep forgetting this must be even more difficult for you than it is for me. So please, ask anything you want. I'll try to answer."

The first thing Maggie wanted to ask was *why* it was difficult for him. He was, after all, the one doing the haunting; she was just an innocent victim. But she had to stick to one subject at a time.

"When you were born," she repeated, "was it before the Civil War or after?"

"After," he replied immediately. "Of course, I wasn't born here. Boston, I believe. And I went to the university at Oxford, I remember that quite clearly. I traveled abroad a good deal, and then I discovered the Chesapeake Bay. I quite fell in love with it and decided on the spot that was where I would build my home."

"Were you ever...married?" She was not certain why she hesitated over that last word. But somehow, inexplicably, it made her uncomfortable to think of him as married.

"No, not at all. As a matter of fact, I believe I was considered something of a rake in those days." His full lips curved in fond reminiscence, and Maggie had no trouble at all picturing him as a rake.

He glanced back at her and added quickly, "But I'm sure that wouldn't interest you. To answer your question, no, I never married."

Maggie found his old-fashioned discretion both amusing and endearing. But there was a great deal about him that she found endearing, entrancing and utterly intriguing—and that only added to her confusion.

She cleared her throat. "When did you—umm—pass on?"

"I've truly no idea." He turned his attention back to the stereo set.

"That's not fair," she returned a little snappishly. "You said you'd cooperate."

He looked up at her patiently. "What did you have for breakfast on your twelfth birthday?"

She scowled. "What? I don't know. How am I supposed to remember a thing like that?"

"Quite. And that was what—a mere ten or fifteen years ago? I have well over a hundred years to recall. I can't be expected to remember every detail."

"Dying is hardly a detail!"

He shrugged and bent to examine the wires on the back of the stereo set. "Perhaps not to you."

Maggie hesitated, somewhat taken aback by this new and unprecedented view of life and death. If ever, by some strange twist of circumstance, she had been in a position to wonder what an encounter with a ghost would be like—which she most certainly had never done—she was positive she would not have imagined anything like this.

"But since then," she ventured, deciding to abandon the subject of his death for the moment, "you've just been...lurking about in that house, watching people?"

"More or less. Sometimes I grew bored and didn't watch at all. There was one family, early on, who had children, and they were entertaining. There was another couple who had a marvelous book collection, and I occupied myself with those for a time."

Maggie's eyes widened. "You read books?"

"Well, of course." Her reaction seemed to surprise him. "What else was there to do?"

"You tell me," she invited weakly.

He walked over to the magazine stand, chose a magazine and stood flipping through it idly as he spoke. "And then there was the old man—I don't know why I keep calling him that, for he wasn't old when he moved in. I suppose because he always acted old. As I said, he had a television set, and I enjoyed that enormously for a time. But he was something of a recluse. Never had anyone in, never did much at all except putter in the garden and pore over maps, planning the trip he was always going to take but never did. It was rather sad, really. After a while ennui simply overcame me and I dozed, off and on, until you came in."

Maggie blinked. "Dozed?"

He looked up, as though his own choice of words puzzled him. "Why, yes. I don't know any other way to describe it. I grow tired or disinterested, and the decades begin to blur together."

"What is the last thing you remember?" Maggie inquired curiously.

"Before you?" He thought back. "There was a television program about a young boy and his dog. A collie, I believe."

"*Lassie*?"

"Yes, that's right."

"That was in the fifties," Maggie said wonderingly.

That was before she was born. She found the entire concept a little mind-boggling and decided it was best not to dwell on it. She pointed out instead, "You missed color television."

His eyes lit up. "They transmit in color now? I always wondered how that could be managed!" He turned eagerly toward the television set. "May I see?"

"In a minute. You promised to answer my questions."

He looked as though he would argue, then reluctantly agreed. "So I did."

But he didn't seem interested in complying, because as soon as he turned away from the television, his attention was caught again by the magazine. Maggie couldn't help wondering how it would look to innocent observers. Would they see a magazine floating in the air, its pages turning slowly? Would they see nothing at all? Was *Maggie* seeing anything at all?

"Do all—departed spirits do that sort of thing? Just sort of hang around and watch us?" She could not help thinking of Aunt Hilly. Was the dear old woman, with that ineffable twinkle in her eye, at this moment watching her favorite niece have a conversation with a ghost? Maggie cast an uneasy glance over her shoulder.

"How should I know?" Christopher replied absently. "I am only responsible for myself." He held the magazine up, open to an advertisement of a male model in a leather jacket, white silk shirt and baggy, multi-pocketed cotton pants. ''Is this what young men are wearing today?''

''Some of them,'' Maggie replied impatiently. ''What I want to know is—''

''And that ensemble you're wearing, is it fashionable as well?'

Distracted, Maggie glanced down at her mismatch of cotton and wool, orange and green. ''Well ... I suppose. It doesn't really matter, it's comfortable—''

''I see.'' He nodded sagely. ''As an academic, you can't be expected to be at the height of fashion.'' He turned the page and glanced from the magazine to Maggie and back again. ''There seems to be something of a discrepancy here.''

He had found a picture of a young woman in a tight black minidress, displaying a great deal of bosom and derriere and a cocky smile. ''Surely this can't be proper.''

''Maybe not,'' Maggie admitted, wondering what it must be like to see a woman's thighs after almost a century. ''But it's in fashion.''

''Do ladies actually roam the streets attired this way?''

Maggie repressed a smile. ''Sometimes.''

''Fascinating,'' he murmured, studying the photograph. ''I do believe I'm going to like this century, after all.''

Maggie chuckled. ''I wouldn't be surprised.''

The burning questions she wanted to ask had lost some of their import in the last few minutes, and it wasn't hard to understand why. It was difficult to discuss matters of esoteric philosophy with a man whose attention was focused on a fashion model, and, really, what did it matter? The answers she got were ridiculous or vague, and the effort of trying to make sense of it all was beginning to give her a headache. He was a ghost, after all—and even *that* had yet to be proved to Maggie's satisfaction. Nothing he said or did could possibly make a difference in the overall scheme of things. She was exhausting herself for no reason.

Maggie walked over to the sofa and picked up the remote control, aiming it at the television. "This device," she explained, "sends a signal to the receiver, which turns the television on or off—" She demonstrated, and the light in Christopher's eyes quickened as he watched "—changes the channels—" His eyes widened. "Or the volume without you ever having to leave your seat."

"Incredible," he murmured. "And look, it *is* color. Imagine that."

Maggie placed the remote control on the end table by the sofa, and Christopher dragged his attention away from the television with obvious difficulty. "Excuse me," he said, "I am taking up too much of your time. What is it that you usually do this time of day?"

Maggie found his sudden consideration a little surprising, to say the least. "Well, I have some papers to grade, and then I guess I'll fix some dinner..."

"Please, don't let me stop you." He waved her away and picked up the remote control, sinking onto the sofa with his eyes focused on the television. "Go right ahead with whatever you normally do, and I'll just sit here quietly out of the way."

Maggie felt as though she had been summarily dismissed, but she couldn't help grinning as she watched him operate the remote control with the fascination of a child, exclaiming softly to himself over the number of channels and the clearness of the picture. After a while he settled on the evening news, and Maggie went into the kitchen to put the groceries away.

"This has got to be the weirdest evening I've ever spent," she muttered. "A ghost is watching television in my living room, I'm acting like nothing unusual is happening at all and, what's more, I'm talking to myself about it."

"So much crime and violence," Christopher commented. "I really would have expected society to have reached a better state of affairs by now."

"I don't think things are really that bad," Maggie said. "We just hear more of it now."

"I suppose."

He was silent then, watching the commercials with the same absorbed attention with which he focused on the news, and after a while Maggie gave up trying to understand what it all must sound like to a man who hadn't heard a news broadcast in at least thirty years. If nothing else, she decided, this entire experience had certainly given her a new way of looking at things...and a great deal to think about.

As the program ended Christopher murmured, "So much information. However do you keep up with it all? It's really quite exhausting."

Maggie was chopping vegetables for dinner—not because she was hungry, but because there was a certain comfort in keeping her hands busy with routine work. If she thought *too* much about what was happening, she really would go mad.

"Well, you don't try to keep up with all of it," she answered, "just the parts that apply to you. Although I guess it must seem a little overwhelming to someone who hasn't been around in—well, however many years you haven't been around. It would really answer a lot of questions, you know, if I knew exactly how long you've been out of touch, if you know what I mean. If you could just tell me your birthdate, for instance..."

She turned, hoping that now that his curiosity was satisfied about the state of the world, he would be more inclined to satisfy some of her curiosity about *his* state. And she stopped in midsentence.

Christopher was gone.

Chapter Four

MAGGIE SPENT a restless night and awoke the next morning hoping that she would be able to convince herself that the events of the afternoon before had been no more than a nightmare. But she had no such luck. Maggie Castle knew herself far too well, and was much too comfortable with what she knew, to experience serious self-doubt about anything of consequence. That innate self-confidence had carried her through life's most demanding challenges without a visible scar, and it would not fail her now—although Maggie almost wished it would. It would be much easier to explain away her unearthly encounter as the result of an unstable temperament, an overwrought imagination or PMS. Maggie was prone to none of those conditions.

She had spent the evening trying to occupy herself with useful, routine things, but had found herself unable to concentrate for more than a few minutes at a time. Straining at shadows, starting at the most innocuous sounds, unable to even watch television for fear she would look up and discover the sounds and sights of modern technology had lured Christopher back, Maggie had finally given up in exasperation and gone to bed early. But she slept fitfully and dreamed of soft brown eyes and an entrancing smile, and she was never quite sure she was dreaming at all.

But the crisp morning sun washed the night away and left no trace of uneasiness in its wake. Maggie awoke to the glare of light streaming through the sheer paneled curtains and bouncing off her stark white bedroom walls, and everything was different. Although she could not begin to try to convince herself none of it had ever happened, it was over now. The day was fresh and new and everything was back to normal.

Maggie was a morning person. She awoke abruptly, clearheaded and energized, and went about the business of the day briskly and efficiently—a characteristic that had cost her more than one roommate and had driven her mother to distraction. By seven-thirty she had made the bed, spent twenty minutes on her exercise bike, showered and made coffee. While an English muffin was heating in the toaster oven and she was standing before the closet, drying her short hair with her fingers and trying to decide what to wear, the telephone rang.

Larry's voice surprised her. "What are you doing calling people this time of day?" she greeted him.

"Fine thanks I get for getting up bright and early to call the Petersons in Michigan. They leave for work before seven, apparently."

For a moment she didn't know what he was talking about. When it registered, Maggie experienced a dim sense of amazement, for it seemed like years instead of mere hours since she and Larry had walked through the house on Walnut Street and he had told her that the owners lived in Michigan. Everything had changed since then . . . and nothing had.

She said somewhat vaguely, "Oh . . . the people who own my house."

"Yeah. I couldn't get hold of them last night, or I would have called you sooner. Anyway, I presented your offer and, though it took some doing, I finally persuaded them to take it.''

That made Maggie smile. She knew the salesman in Larry well enough to realize the Petersons had probably snapped up her offer and were glad to get it. But she couldn't fault him for a little artful exaggeration; that, after all, was the nature of his business.

''There's only one condition,'' he added. ''It has to be an as-is sale.''

''What does that mean?''

''No warranty, explicit or implied. It's not unusual, honey, when you're talking about a house that old. It simply means the sellers won't be responsible if the roof collapses a month after you move in. For your own protection, though, I'd have a building inspector in before you make a final commitment.''

''Sure,'' she replied absently, ''whatever you think. Larry, about the house...''

He was quick to pick up on the disturbance in her tone: ''Having second thoughts?''

''No. I was just wondering...how much do you know about it?''

''Like what?''

''Well...'' She wound the telephone cord around her finger, choosing her words carefully. ''Like how old it is, and who built it and...'' It took all her self-restraint not to add *whether or not anyone ever died there*. But Larry would be sure to demand an explanation for a question like that, and she certainly wasn't ready to provide one. So she finished simply, ''You know, the history of the place.''

''Well, nothing really. It just came to me through the estate lawyers, you know that. I suppose,'' he offered reluctantly, "I could look it up in the Hall of Records, if it's important."

"I'd appreciate that." And she smiled, lightening her voice. "It'll give your secretary something to do."

He grunted. "I'll be sure to tell her you said so. Listen, the best way to handle this is to go ahead and draw up a contract now, contingent on the building inspector. That way, if we find any structural defects you'll still have an out, but no one can edge in with an offer in the meantime. If you're sure," he added, "that you want to go through with this."

"I gave you a check," she reminded him. "You made the offer to your clients. That's a deal, isn't it?"

"There are always loopholes, my dear. And for you, I'd make a point of finding them." And then his voice changed. "You *are* having second thoughts, aren't you?"

"No," she assured him quickly, and she meant it. Ghost or no ghost, the house was hers, and nothing could change that. In some strange way her discovery of Christopher Durand had made her even more possessive of the house, as though the strange visitation, or whatever it had been, had sealed the deal in a more permanent way than a mere cash deposit could ever do. Of all the people who had lived in that house, which of them could say they had actually met the builder? Could that house ever be more special to anyone than it was to her?

"No," she repeated, "I'm not having second thoughts. It's just that this is probably the biggest decision I've ever made, and it's a little overwhelming. Exciting, but overwhelming. You won't let anything go wrong, will you?" she added anxiously.

She could almost see him relax. She had no doubt that Larry would have broken every rule in the book to help her out if she had changed her mind, but she also knew that he hoped he didn't have to. A deal was a deal, and he had a reputation to maintain.

"Nothing that's in my power to prevent," he assured her. "I can have the contract for you this afternoon. Shall we have dinner?"

She hesitated. She had papers to grade, lessons to prepare and work on her thesis to do. She had lost an entire afternoon and evening yesterday, and she really didn't feel like being witty and charming tonight. On the other hand, it *was* awfully sweet of Larry to do all this for her—selling her a house he really didn't want her to have, taking less than he probably could have gotten from another buyer, then going to all the trouble of rushing the contracts through. She owed him something for that.

And, all things considered, it probably wasn't a good idea for her to be alone in the apartment tonight. Company might be nice.

"Sure," she agreed, and then surprised herself by adding, "I'll cook."

"Can't wait. Seven?"

"Great. See you then. And bring the contract," she added quickly, just before he hung up.

Her first class wasn't until ten-thirty, but Maggie wanted to spend some time on the computer before then. Until that moment she had not consciously decided to pursue the mystery of Christopher Durand further, just as she had not really intended to ask Larry to look into the history of the house. But she knew she couldn't just let the matter drop. Even if the whole thing turned out to be nothing but a wild-goose chase, a fan-

four-year colleges; it was ranked among the top five percent of junior colleges in the nation. Funded by both the state university system and local, private sources, Leeland was able to offer state-of-the-art equipment and some of the finest instructors available. Maggie had chosen Leeland both for its reputation and for its policy of flexible class loads for instructors who were doing post-graduate work. But if she were totally honest with herself, Maggie would have to admit that the biggest attraction Leeland held for her was its computer system.

The Leeland computer was linked to the university network, which was in turn linked to state and local research facilities, the Library of Congress and various other information-gathering facilities across the nation. Fax transmissions could be received almost instantaneously, or hard copies of data could be requested by mail. Although none of this was particularly unusual for a four-year college or a university, such facilities were not usually found in a junior college. Leeland used that fringe benefit to recruit instructors from the pool of graduates to whom such a facility would be invaluable in completing their masters and doctoral work. But for Maggie, like so many other working students to whom higher education meant a constant juggling of time and money, the biggest drawing point was that computer time was free to Leeland staff members. And she was not in the least hesitant to take advantage of the college's generosity.

She escaped the departmental meeting with no more than a mild reprimand from Dr. Brooks and at ten o'clock was elated to find an opening on the computer. She slipped into a cubicle, typed in her ID number and immediately entered a request for a network search.

With so little to go on, she had to adopt a hit-or-miss policy, so at the prompt she typed simply, *Biography: Durand, Christopher*.

The computer returned, *Narrow search*.

She thought a minute. Hadn't he said something about her house being completed in 1895? She didn't know a better place to begin, so she responded simply, *Circa 1895*.

The screen blinked and the system purred for a minute, then the prompt returned, *Narrow search*.

"All right," Maggie muttered, "so you're not going to make this easy."

She cleared her previous entries and began from the top. *Architecture (Chesapeake Bay, Maryland OR Germany): Biography: Durand, Christopher*, and then she hesitated. He had said he was born after the Civil War, so to be on the safe side she typed in *Circa 1865*. And to allow for the vagaries of a ghost's memory and the possible life span of the person in question, she added, *through 1955, inclusive*.

The computer whirred and the screen blinked. *Searching*.

Maggie leaned back and sipped from her Styrofoam cup of coffee, appreciating the irony of the fact that she was using a computer to confirm or deny the existence of a ghost. This was twentieth-century technology confronting ancient superstition in the most basic and dramatic way. She didn't really expect to find anything, and she didn't know why she was trying, except that she had never been the type of person to leave a project half finished.

There was no doubt in her mind that she had experienced something very unusual yesterday. Whether or not that experience had anything to do with the supernatural was still open for debate in her mind. As for Christopher Durand's having been an actual person who lived and died sometime in the past . . . well, that presented an even bigger question. She knew that there were people who made full-time careers of researching paranormal events, and she wasn't certain what methods they used. But Maggie required a bit more than the word of a ghost to prove the existence of such things, and the computer seemed as good a place to start as any.

The beeping of the computer startled her so badly that she sloshed coffee onto her hand. The screen reported, *(3) items found. Enter choice.*

"Good heavens," Maggie murmured. Absently wiping the lukewarm coffee from her hand with the hem of her sweater, she leaned forward and entered the command *View*. The first item scrolled onto the screen.

Durand, Christopher Alan (1869-1899) A scholar and architect of minor import most known for his artful incorporation of modern innovations into traditional designs. Belonging to the group of "progressive intellectuals" of the late nineteenth century that included Sigmund Freud and H. G. Wells, Durand is mentioned in the later letters of Jules Verne.

Maggie swallowed hard. All right, she told herself. All this proved was that a man named Christopher Durand had actually existed once upon a time, that he had been an architect of minor import and that he had hung out with some fairly well-known people. It did *not* prove that the man she had spent a good part of yesterday afternoon and evening with was the disembodied spirit of that same Christopher Durand.

And if one were completely logical about it, taking into consideration all the millions upon millions of people who had lived and died since time began, what were the chances—assuming one accepted the possibility at all—of encountering the ghost of a person who just happened to have his biography written up in an encyclopedia? That was exactly the kind of coincidental claptrap devotees of the supernatural always conveniently ignored and that annoyed Maggie to no end. Why was it always Beethoven or Cleopatra or Elvis who managed to get messages across from the other side? Why wasn't it ever Joe the tailor or Mary the housewife? All in all, Maggie decided somewhat petulantly, this biographical entry argued more *against* the authenticity of Christopher Durand than for it.

But her heart was beating hard as she entered the command to view the next item.

Durand, Christopher
Unique Homes of Europe, by Theodore Artweiler, 1932 Appletone Press

The residence of Baron von Holstedler, designed in 1888 by Christopher Durand, features as its central support a live oak tree. Measuring thirty feet in diameter at the base and . . .

Maggie had to stop reading. Her eyes literally could not focus and she kept hearing Christopher's voice in the back of her head, negligently recounting, *I once designed a house built entirely around a tree. . . . I admit, it was a bit eccentric. But so was the gentleman who commissioned it—a baron, I believe.*

Maggie took a deep breath. She sipped her coffee. She murmured, "Weird."

And that was exactly how she felt—weird. Yesterday she had had a conversation with a man who had an unsettling habit of appearing and disappearing when she wasn't looking, and he had told her about a house he had designed around a tree for a baron. Today she found documented evidence of that very same house. This article no more proved the existence of ghosts than the last one had; Maggie knew that. Then why was she finding it increasingly difficult to remain skeptical?

On the other hand, how much more convincing did she need?

She scanned the article, caring little about floating staircases and advanced drainage systems, and learned that the house, at the time of the article's publication in 1932, was not open to the public. She called up the next entry.

Durand, Christopher
The Compleat Compendium of Architects of the Nineteenth Century, compiled by S. S. Lauder
1961 University Press

Durand, Christopher (1869-1899) Born in Boston to an affluent railroad family, Durand was educated at Oxford University. After several years traveling in Europe, he returned to the United States and studied briefly under Louis H. Sullivan, famed for his development of the skyscraper. Sullivan considered him unpromising, however, and after a year, Durand returned to Europe, where he soon acquired other interests. Known as an eccentric among his peers, Durand spent some time immersed in the developing technology of the day and developing his own inventions, none of which were ever patented.

Durand's early efforts in building design met with discouragement, being variously cited as "unsightly," "defying the laws of gravity" and "unsound." It was perhaps this criticism that modified Durand's brilliance into more conservative designs, and the acclaim he finally achieved was for the simplicity and structural solidity of his designs.

In 1890, Durand experimented successfully with the collection of solar energy and designed the first active-solar building in Charleston, South Carolina. Although earthquake proof, the house was destroyed by fire as a result of aftershocks from the earthquake in 1886.

In 1895, Durand retired to the Chesapeake Bay area of Maryland, where he lived until his death at the age of thirty.

Maggie scanned the material quickly, and then caught her breath. At the bottom of her screen was the single notation, *Photo*.

The graphics capability of the computer screen did not allow it to receive photographs, so the system thoughtfully provided the user with the reminder that a photograph could be obtained through hard copy or facsimile. Maggie hastily placed an order for a facsimile and hurried to the fax machine in the outer room to await delivery.

She hardly noticed the other people in the room—teachers, administrative and clerical personnel engaged in the ordinary activities that kept any educational institution running properly. The copy machine hummed, staplers clicked and voices conversed back and forth. A few people greeted Maggie, and she returned their smiles nervously. She stood before the fax machine like a mother hovering over its young, twisting her hands together anxiously.

She was about to rush back to her terminal to make sure she had entered her request properly when the machine began to purr. Maggie snatched up the sheet of paper that was delivered before it even had a chance to cool, and some instinct made her hurry back to the privacy of her cubicle before examining it.

And there it was, a two-by-three-inch black-and-white reproduction of a photograph of Durand, Christopher, 1869-1899. Dark, soulful eyes. Sleek brown hair combed back from his face but tumbling forward slightly in the photograph, just as it had done in her living room last night. The arresting features of a sinfully beautiful face: high cheekbones, sharp nose, full, sensuous lips. In the photograph he was wearing a high-collared shirt, a dark coat and a wide, old-fashioned tie. But there was no mistaking that face. It had first greeted her from the shadows of the house on Walnut Street, had lighted with excitement as he explored her kitchen and had gone rapt with fascination as he watched her television. It was the face of a man who had been dead for almost a hundred years.

Maggie sank slowly to her chair, the paper still clutched in both hands. *So,* she thought distantly, *there you have it. Proof.*

Her heart was beating with a rapid, skipping cadence, but inside she felt very relaxed, almost calm. She had seen evidence of his paranormal abilities with her own eyes. She had checked his story against hard data, and now she held in her hands unmistakable identification. There was no more room for doubt. She had actually met a ghost.

Another person, even with the evidence staring her in the face, would have had difficulty accepting what she had believed all her life to be patently impossible. But Maggie's ability to adapt to changing circumstances with ease and alacrity was one of her greatest assets, both as a scientist and a woman. And the greatest asset a scientist could have was a capacity for entertaining the impossible. Even in the ordered, dependable world of mathematics there were mysteries, possibilities, speculations . . . and it was from those possibilities that Maggie received her most exciting challenges, her greatest satisfactions. There was an answer to everything. As Sherlock Holmes once had said, "When you have eliminated the impossible, whatever remains, *however improbable*, must be the truth." Maggie knew when to stop searching for impossibilities and accept the improbable.

For a brief moment, the paper shook in her hand and she breathed shallowly. How could this have happened to her? Who would ever imagine that of all people something like this should happen to *her*? She wanted to tell someone. She should publish a paper. What a discovery she had made! She should tell the world—and who would ever believe her?

That last question was only one reason why the urge to shout her discovery at the top of her lungs left her almost at once. The truth was that what had happened to her was incredible, monumental and utterly stupendous, but it affected no one but her. And it was over.

Deliberately, she regulated her breathing, and her hands almost stopped shaking. She concentrated on putting things into perspective. Amazing? Yes. Note-worthy? Undoubtedly. But for public consumption? Hardly.

One day when she was old, idle or in a contemplative mood, she would look back on all this and try to discern what significance it had for her life. But for now all she could really say was that one entire afternoon and evening of her life had been given over to a singularly remarkable occurrence, one that few people, if any, had ever experienced before, and one that was not likely to happen again, at least not to her. She wished now that she had not wasted so much time on skepticism, for there were so many questions she should have asked him, so many observations she should have made.... She wished, in fact, that she had paid closer attention, to better catalog the experience for memory. But regrets were useless, and Maggie was not the type of person to dwell on things she could not change.

She looked at the photograph in her hand and shook her head slowly. She had to say it out loud, softly, just once. "Incredible. Absolutely incredible."

"Remarkable," echoed a voice over her shoulder. "A splendid likeness."

Maggie spun in her chair and almost fell out of it when she saw Christopher Durand.

Chapter Five

HE WAS WEARING a loose, white silk shirt, stylishly baggy gray pants and a leather jacket with the sleeves pushed up. He looked as though he had just stepped out of a current Italian fashion magazine. He looked sexy and wickedly handsome. He looked like the kind of man screaming teenage girls threw their underpants onstage for, the kind middle-aged women had total body lifts for.... He was every woman's fantasy, and he was standing not six inches away from Maggie. The very space around her seemed to be charged with the vividness of his presence.

Air rushed back into her lungs with a gulp, but even then she could not speak. She looked from him to the photo and then back again, almost as though to reassure herself that it *was* the same person, that there was no mistake....

There was no mistake.

"You!" she gasped at last. "Where have you— How did you— I thought you were gone!"

"So I was," he admitted with a shrug, "for a while. Now I'm back. Tell me—" His dark brows knitted with concentration as he eyed the paper she held, and he placed one hand on the back of her chair. Instinctively Maggie edged away. "—That photograph—how did you make it so small? Is that a newspaper in your hand? Have they changed that much?"

"It's a copy," she responded automatically. "A facsimile transmission, actually, but please don't ask me what that is or how it works."

With a sudden disarming grin he agreed, "All right, I won't." He perched upon the edge of the desk beside her terminal. "So. You've been delving into my past, have you?"

She couldn't take her eyes off the way his booted feet swung in a casual rhythm a few inches above the floor, the way he braced his palms against the desk as though for support, the way the narrow waistband of his trousers defined his form. So real, so...lifelike. Even his shirt was open one button, affording her a glimpse of his collarbone and the faintest shading of dark hair.

"Umm...yes," she managed, after a moment.

"And?"

She looked at him blankly.

"What did you find out?"

And yet, she decided studiously, as perfect an imitation of a real-life man as he projected, it *was* possible to see it was only an imitation. Not, strangely enough, because anything was missing or less than normal. Instead, it was because he was so perfect, so larger than life, so...intense. He not only took up space with his presence, he energized all the space around him, an effect that was much stronger and more dynamic today than it had been yesterday. It was as though every molecule and particle within his range responded in some subtle way to him, shifting just slightly, moving a fraction faster, burning a touch brighter.... Even the atoms of Maggie's body seemed to register the change, like a low electric thrum that was titillating even as it was disconcerting. There was power in him today, vibrancy, expectancy. . . life. If he were a color, Maggie decided irrationally, today he would be electric blue.

She brought herself back to focus on his question. "I found out that everything you told me was true," she answered simply. "You are a ghost."

He winced a little. "I wish you wouldn't use that word. It's not very flattering."

And then he looked at her, clear-eyed and curious. "You don't seem very unsettled by the fact. Yesterday you were more than a little skeptical, and today you're convinced. I must say, I'm not sure *I* would react as well, if the circumstances were reversed. Aren't you having any trouble at all accepting this? Don't you want to thrash it about for a while?"

"Not really," Maggie answered slowly. "There are a lot of things in this world I can't explain, but I accept. A lot of things I don't have to see to believe in."

"But you're a scientist," he pointed out.

"Exactly. I believe in quarks. Why can't I believe in ghosts?"

He nodded, his eyes glinting with approval. "I admire the way you think. Rational but even-minded, the sign of a great achiever." And then he cocked his head curiously. "What are quarks?"

Maggie smiled, pleased that there were things she could teach even a self-confessed genius. "Mostly they're a figment of the physicist's imagination. Supposedly, they're the basic constituent of matter— smaller than protons or neutrons. But the only evidence for their existence is mathematical supposition."

"Deductive reasoning," he supplied, and looked for all the world as though he understood what she was talking about.

"More or less. No one has ever seen one, but their existence would explain a lot of things."

He smiled. "Just like me. You *are* a clear thinker."

Maggie was not at all certain she could pursue that line of reasoning. She did not feel as though she was thinking very clearly at all. She said instead, cautiously, "You look different today. Your clothes..."

He seemed pleased that she had noticed. "The height of fashion. I've always taken pride in my appearance."

"But..." No, she didn't want to get into that. How a ghost managed to change his clothes, why he would want to... She had a feeling that if she asked, he would tell her, and she had reached her limit of endurance for the day by simply accepting the fact that he existed.

"Oh, good heavens!" She glanced at her watch with a jolt. "I have a class in two minutes!"

She hurriedly began to gather up her notes and empty coffee cup, clearing the terminal for the next user. Christopher watched her alertly. "What is this machine?"

"A computer." The minute she answered she regretted it. She simply was not prepared to explain the computer age to a ghost in a few concise sentences.

"What does it do?"

"A lot of things. It's an information-retrieval system, mostly."

Whatever hope she might have had of satisfying him with that answer was dashed with his next, predictable question. "How does it work?"

"Binary numbers, electronic encoding... I really don't have time to explain it to you now." She swung the strap of her purse over her shoulder and searched beneath the desk for her briefcase. She was certain she had brought it with her—or had she left it at the staff meeting? Had she had it in her hand when she left the apartment this morning? She couldn't remember.

"I understand." He bent to examine the back of the monitor. "You don't mind if I study it on my own?"

"I certainly do! One wrong move and you could blow the whole system." Come to think of it, with his supernatural powers he might be able to do more than just blow the system. Who could say what would happen when ectoplasm mixed with data banks?

"Blow," he repeated. "As in wind?"

"As in destroy." She lifted a stack of print-out paper and knelt to examine the space between the desk and the wall. No briefcase was lodged there.

"I certainly wouldn't want to take a chance on blowing the system," he agreed gravely. "Perhaps there's a technical manual I could study?"

"Go to the library," she advised, and then straightened up, pushing her hair out of her eyes and looking around the small space in frustration. Her class notes and textbooks were in that briefcase.

"Is this what you're looking for?"

Christopher reached down and lifted her briefcase from the top of the trash can, and she snatched it from him gratefully. "Yes!"

She fled from the cubicle in a rush and was almost to the door of the computer room before it occurred to her to wonder what would become of Christopher when she left. She hurried back, but the cubicle was empty. She didn't have time to feel frustrated—she was already five minutes late for her class.

MAGGIE WAS GIFTED—or perhaps cursed, depending on the point of view—with the predisposition for strict linear thinking compounded by a touch of tunnel vision. It was impossible for her to worry about more than one thing at a time or to concentrate with any degree of effectiveness on anything other than what she happened to be doing at the moment. She forgot appointments, misplaced keys and lost her briefcase. But in the classroom, at the computer or in the laboratory, she was brilliant. She focused on one thing at a time, gave it her full attention and let incidentals fall by the wayside.

It was habit, therefore, more than desire or will that allowed her to push Christopher Durand to the back of her mind. By the time she reached her ten-thirty class at 10:42, she was thinking about nothing other than the lesson she had prepared. Everything about Christopher Durand, from wonder to curiosity to the dozens of specific questions that were rattling around in her mind, formed a waiting list to be examined later.

Although teaching was a means to an end for Maggie, a way to pay the bills until she received the enormous research grant that was surely in her future and settled down to win the Nobel Prize for her work in artificial intelligence—or, perhaps, for the production of final, indisputable evidence of the existence of quarks— she *did* enjoy her class time. The students at Leeland were for the most part ambitious about their studies and took their course load seriously. Many of them were paying their own tuition through full- or part-time jobs and knew the value of every minute spent in class. For that reason Maggie tried hard never to be late, and she apologized profusely for the lapse today before launching immediately into the lesson.

The class was Freshman Algebra, a required course for every student at Leeland. Maggie did not fool herself that any of the twenty-odd students gathered in the room shared her passion for the subject. She always devoted a little extra effort to making the class interesting, both for her students' sakes and her own. When the required course material had been covered and she could feel the class's attention begin to wander, she took off her glasses, leaned against her desk and announced, "Okay, now the fun part. How many of you were able to figure out that the puzzle I gave you last time was really a geometric progression?"

One of the male students answered, "That part was easy. What I couldn't figure out was how to work it."

There were some laughs and murmurs of agreement, and Maggie turned to the board. "Boy, are you guys going to feel silly."

As she began to recreate the problem on the board, one of the girls commented, "Look at that, she's not even using a book. How can you remember all those numbers?"

"Some people never forget a face," Maggie quipped in return. "I never forget a number." She liked the relaxed atmosphere and easy repartee that was characteristic of all her classes. No one could work well in a repressive environment.

"What I want to know," someone else said, "is who invents all this stuff."

"The same guy that makes up the *Times* crossword puzzles," came the reply from the back of the room.

"No, I mean the whole system. Who was crazy enough to sit down one day and think up mathematics?"

"Ms Castle," someone teased, and Maggie grinned, still writing on the board.

"Think back a little further," she advised.

"The Babylonians," said a girl in the front row. "Everyone knows that."

"The Atlanteans," wisecracked someone else.

"Actually," Maggie said, finishing the problem and beginning the solution, "you can probably go back further than that. Mathematics is a part of nature. The movement of the stars, the rising and setting of the sun and moon, the changing of the seasons, all those were very important to ancient man. What we call math today was probably just common sense to the caveman, a matter of survival."

"If you're telling me that a caveman would have a better chance of understanding this stuff than I do..."

"I'm telling you that there are mathematical relationships in everything you examine," Maggie replied. "Like music, which is nothing more than a series of mathematical progressions—"

"And possibly the oldest form of communication known to man," supplied a familiar voice.

The chalk snapped in Maggie's hand with a squeaking sound, and she swung her head around. Christopher Durand was leaning against the windowsill, his arms and his ankles crossed casually, awash in a brilliant spray of sunlight. She blinked, opened her mouth to exclaim in astonishment and swallowed the sound just in time. She cast a surreptitious glance around to see if anyone else had noticed anything unusual. All she saw were curious faces focused on her, waiting for her to finish her sentence.

"P-possibly the oldest form of communication known to man," Maggie repeated, although that was not at all what she had intended to say. She turned back to the board and concentrated hard on completing the problem with the broken piece of chalk, trying to make her voice sound normal. "Even in the growth pattern of the petals of a common flower, which is exactly—" she made a final notation and turned around, trying for a brilliant smile but managing only a nervous one "—what this puzzle demonstrates. Does everyone see how easy that was? Isn't that great?"

But while the murmurs of appreciation—and a few of confusion—went around the room, Maggie looked distractedly back at Christopher. He smiled at her pleasantly and innocently, just as though he had every right to be there. "Your students look older than you do," he commented, moving away from the window. "How old are you, anyway?"

"Twenty-eight," she responded automatically, and Charles, in the desk nearest to her, looked up curiously.

"Twenty-eight what?" he asked.

Maggie could have bitten her tongue. She would *not* be reduced to the stereotypical heroine of every ghost movie she had ever seen, chattering away to thin air while the people around her made plans to have her committed. But what was he doing in her classroom? The house she could understand. Even her apartment, the computer room . . . but *not* her classroom.

"Twenty-eight possible variations to this puzzle," she lied to Charles blithely.

Christopher clucked his tongue reprovingly. "There's only one answer, and you know it," he told her.

Maggie half turned toward the blackboard and beneath the cover of the voices of her students she muttered, "They can't see you, can they?"

He glanced around, unconcerned. "Apparently not."

"What are you doing here?" she whispered furiously. "You shouldn't be here, you have no right—"

She caught herself just as her voice began to rise and took a deep breath.

"All right, class," she said loudly, turning. "What do you think will happen if we reduce this answer exponentially?"

"We'll get the same thing we started out with," answered Charles, her brightest student.

Christopher chuckled. "He's in for a surprise."

Maggie spared him a quelling glance. "Let's try it."

She focused intently on working the familiar problem. It was not easy to do, however, with Christopher standing so close and watching her every move. Her heart was racing and her face was flushed, and she was annoyed with the physical reactions she couldn't control. Self-consciousness was only part of it; a greater part was what he stirred in her simply by being near. She was aware of him; no one else was. It was exciting, troubling and . . . stimulating.

"Seven," Christopher said quietly.

The chalk snapped again, leaving barely a nub with which to finish the equation. Maggie shot a startled glance at him.

"You made an error," he pointed out. "You wrote nine."

Maggie hastily erased the nine with the palm of her hand and wrote a seven.

"There." He nodded approvingly. "Just reduce that sum by a factor of nine . . ."

"I know how to do it," she muttered.

Quickly, almost too rapidly for her students to grasp, Maggie finished the problem and turned with a bright, blatantly false smile. "There, you see," she announced, dusting her hands. "Not everything is what it appears to be. Even in math there is always room for surprise."

"Hear, hear," murmured Christopher.

"How did you do that?" demanded Charles, and there were murmurs of dissent and confusion from all around the room. "That can't be right."

This was exactly the kind of curiosity that Maggie liked to pique, and on another occasion she would have made the most of it. Today, however, she merely replied, "Extra credit for anyone who can duplicate these results on his own." She began to erase the board before the students could copy her work. "Class dismissed."

As the class dissolved around her, Maggie took out her frustration on the eraser and blackboard, applying more energy than was necessary to the task. She was almost as angry with herself as with Christopher. Nothing had ever interfered with her class time before. Nothing. But how could she be expected to concentrate with an invisible being peering over her shoulder, providing unheard advice and unwanted interference?

"You are a very good teacher," Christopher complimented her. "I almost wish I had had someone like you when I was in university, though I doubt I should have done as well." He shook his head in wonder. "A lady professor. Who could have imagined? It's bound to be distracting."

Maggie stacked her books into her briefcase, slammed it shut and started for the door. Grim faced, she pushed through the congestion of the lunchtime class change outside her door and negotiated her way through the hall. Christopher kept in step.

"You seem upset," he commented.

Maggie willfully held back her retort, aware of the hundreds of eyes and ears that would be quick to focus on a young math instructor talking to herself—worse yet, yelling at herself. Instead she headed for the front door, digging in her oversize purse for the crumpled beret she always kept ready to protect her hair from the wind. Jerking the hat down over her curls, she pushed open the door and stalked out into the bright day.

For all her slightness of build, Maggie could imitate the stance of a linebacker when she was agitated, and she was agitated now. Her head lowered against the gusting autumn wind, her shoulders hunched purposefully and her stride long and indomitable, she dodged oncomers, brushed past obstacles and cut corners, looking neither left nor right.

"I wonder if it was something I said," Christopher murmured.

Maggie slowed her step only when she reached a relatively deserted covered walkway that led toward the fine arts building. She waited until a couple of students strolled by, nodding distractedly when they glanced at her, and when the walkway was empty she turned on Christopher.

"Ghosts haunt houses," she told him distinctly. "Castle dungeons, graveyards, the odd moor or two.... They do *not* haunt modern apartment buildings or college campuses or *my classroom*, do you understand?"

"What odd notions you have," he replied casually. His eyes were busily scanning the area beyond her shoulder, registering movement and color, reflecting delight in everything he saw.

Furiously Maggie stepped in front of him, demanding his attention. "You can't do this," she told him. "I refuse to have my life disrupted by a ghost! You've made your point, whatever it is. You've even managed to convince me to believe in you—''

"I had nothing to do with that," he interrupted. "You proved it to yourself in true scientific style."

"But that's enough, already!" Maggie finished adamantly. "Just go away now and leave me alone."

"And where should I go?" he inquired politely, much as he had yesterday when she first met him.

Maggie could have stamped her foot in impatience. "I don't know—I don't care! Wherever it is you're supposed to be—just away from me!"

His eyes danced with merriment, as though he were enjoying a private joke. "But my dear girl, don't you see? I *am* where I belong. You are here, and so am I."

Maggie shook her head in forceful denial. "No, I don't see! How can I see? The only thing I can see is you, and you're a *ghost*!"

He scowled a little in annoyance. "I've asked you not to use that word. It's so vulgar."

Maggie heard footsteps coming up the walkway, and she turned her back, moving away from them. "I don't care what you call yourself," she began in a low undertone. "The point is—"

"Poltergeist," he decided, and his eyes took on a mischievous glint. "It means playful spirit. I find that appropriate, don't you?"

And to prove his point, he snatched her hat off her head and tossed it in the air.

Maggie gave an involuntary squeal as her hat, propelled out of her reach by a gust of wind, sailed across the lawn. She ran to catch it, afraid that if she did not, Christopher would. While she might be able to explain a hat that flew *off* her head, she doubted she would be able to explain one that floated back toward her.

The hat landed a few feet away, and a passing student retrieved it for her. "Some wind today, huh?" he commented. The ease of his friendly grin as he dusted grass and leaves off the felt told her immediately that he had mistaken her for a potential conquest. "Maybe you need someone to walk along and hold you down in case the wind starts to carry *you* away."

Maggie took her hat from him with as much dignity as possible. "Thank you, that won't be necessary."

"It's no trouble," he urged, still grinning.

"I'm not interested," she replied firmly, trying her best to look three inches taller and ten years older.

She pulled the cap tightly down over her wind-tossed curls and kept her gaze cool; after a moment the student shrugged and continued on his way.

Behind her, Christopher burst into laughter. "He was flirting with you!" he exclaimed, delighted. "That young man was actually flirting with you!"

Maggie glowered, her voice low and tight. "I don't see anything so funny about that."

His eyes danced, and his entire form practically shimmered with vivacity. "But that's the trouble—you can't see any of it! It's all so ordinary, so everyday to you, you've no idea what this wonderful world of yours is really like!"

With a sudden burst of energy, Christopher sprinted past her, into the courtyard where students were picnicking, chatting and studying. Maggie could not prevent a gasp as he sprang onto a bench where a boy and a girl sat with a book open between them. They did not even look up.

"Ah, Maggie, just look!" His voice was rich and vibrant, his expression animated, intense with excitement and joy. He spread his arms as though to embrace everything within sight. "Look around you—the colors, the warmth, the brilliance...the *life*. Just look!"

For a moment Maggie was captured by the spell of his enthusiasm, and she did look. The lawn was emerald green and littered with scraps of yellow, red and orange—leaves that lay like abandoned toys on an expensive carpet. The sky was a startling cobalt blue, and the sunshine washed concrete walkways and pillars looked like brilliant white marble. Sitting on the grass, lounging in the shadows, stretched out on the benches with their faces upturned to the sun were healthy young people dressed in vibrant primary colors—red, purple, blue and yellow—laughing, talking, tossing back their gleaming hair. The crisp air was intoxicating, and for that moment—just that brief moment—Maggie saw her world as though for the first time. The beauty and the poignancy of it clutched at her heart.

"Maggie," Christopher said softly, lowering himself to a squatting position on the bench, at eye level with her. His eyes were shining, and as she stepped closer to him she could feel the atmosphere change. Surely this sensation should be discernible to everyone around him, but no one looked up. No one but Maggie noticed anything at all, and Maggie's heart was thrumming in her chest.

"Maggie," he repeated, and his voice seemed to strain with the effort to contain his excitement. "Look at you. You have gold streaks in your hair, and your eyes are violet—not just blue, but as purple as wildflowers. I've never seen eyes quite that color before. The freckles on your nose, that absurd red hat and the way the wind is blowing your curls around... I wish you could know the pleasure I feel simply from looking at you, but I can't even put it into words."

There was a sort of wonder in his eyes as he spoke, almost a reverence in his voice. Maggie's hand went self-consciously to her throat. Had any man ever looked at her like that, spoken to her like that? Everything was new to him, rich with nuance and promise, and to be the focus of that intense admiration was like no feeling Maggie had ever known.

His eyes swept away from her, alight with new discoveries. "These children—" with a wave of his hand he included the young men and women around them "—so young, so healthy and full of energy. So perfect. Men today are stronger and taller than ever, and the women..." Maggie watched as his eyes moved appreciatively over the long legs of the miniskirted young blonde sitting next to him, deep in conversation with her boyfriend. "I never dreamed there could be such beautiful women. And so many of them all in one place!" He let his gaze dance from one attractive female to another.

Following so closely on the heels of the lovely words he had said to her, Maggie found his unabashed display of admiration somewhat irritating, even insulting. She turned abruptly and walked away. As she suspected he would, Christopher followed—although, she couldn't help noticing, at a somewhat more leisurely pace. His eyes busily absorbed everything in his path, but she was certain they lingered with particular appreciation on each passing female form.

She stopped in the privacy of a little-used doorway and turned to him. "What do you care about women, anyway?" she demanded, and though she didn't intend to, she sounded a little snappish. "You're over a hundred and twenty years old!"

His eyes danced. "I'll never be too old to stop looking," he assured her. "Although, of course, it's rather late to do anything more. I've long since outgrown any carnal impulses, I assure you. My interest is purely esthetic."

Maggie clasped her hands together and brought them to her lips, sucking in her breath and trying hard to remain calm. "Listen," she said after a moment, "I want you to try to understand something. It's been hard for me, meeting—well, seeing you. It was hard for me to accept who—what—you are. You said yourself you would have trouble if our positions were reversed, and let me tell you, it's not easy. But that's okay. I can deal with it. What I can't handle is having you pop up all the time, asking crazy questions and getting in my way and—it's driving me crazy, can you understand that?"

She made a somewhat frantic gesture with her arm. Her voice was thinning toward the edge of desperation, but she didn't care. "I have enough trouble keeping my checkbook balanced and my appointment calendar straight and remembering where I left my glasses, and I just can't deal with a ghost in my life! You've got to go away now. You've got to!"

The merriment left his eyes, replaced with an earnest expression that mirrored hers. "Maggie," he said softly. His voice was melodious, mesmerizing—yet hesitant, as though he were searching for words. "For years, centuries, aeons, I've lived in twilight, half aware, knowing but not understanding, watching but not caring. Now I see colors. Now I see *life*, and energy and purpose all around me. How can I leave all this? How could anyone leave it?"

Maggie's throat tightened. The truth was he *had* left it, over ninety years ago. But hearing his words, seeing the yearning on his face and remembering the ecstasy that had radiated from him only moments ago, how could she tell him that? She did understand, in some strange way, and the understanding pricked with poignancy in her chest.

She looked away from him helplessly, rubbing at the base of her skull, where a tension headache was beginning. "But—why me? Can't you go somewhere else, haunt someone else?"

A rather puzzled expression crossed his face. "No," he said slowly, "I don't believe I can. Somehow, in a way I don't understand, I seem only to be able to be where you are." And he frowned a little, thoughtfully. "Odd, isn't it?"

Odd. The word seemed the quintessential understatement—for him, for her, for the world at large. Could it have been a mere twenty-four hours ago that Maggie Castle was just an ordinary woman with ordinary problems, muddling along the best she could? What had she ever done to deserve this? Why was this happening to her?

She looked at him quickly, seizing on one hope. "But last night you went away. Where did you go? Can't you do it again?"

"I didn't go anywhere," he corrected. "I was merely—resting."

And at her blank look, he explained simply, "I must rejuvenate myself, just as you do in sleep. And though I do seem to have a great deal more stamina—" he smiled "—energy, if you will—now, than I ever did before, I still . . . fade out, sometimes."

"Oh, God," Maggie moaned, clutching at the pain in the back of her neck. "I don't understand. I don't want to understand. I just want everything to be normal again."

"Perhaps," suggested Christopher with a note of apology, "I could try to be less—obtrusive."

"Stay out of my classroom," Maggie said forcefully.

"And less demanding," he continued, though he looked dubious. "I don't mean to bring you trouble, but I truly have no more control over this than you do."

She stared at him. "Do you mean you're going to haunt me forever?"

He winced. "I don't like to think of it in that way."

"Forever?" she repeated incredulously.

"I don't know!" For the first time there was a note of exasperation in his voice. "All I know is that I am here and you are here, and the sensible thing to do seems to be to try to make the best of it."

Maggie's head was throbbing, her mind was spinning, and she had absolutely no idea how to respond. After a moment of openmouthed silence, she turned on her heel and walked away, as though by doing so she could leave her problems behind.

Of course, it wasn't as easy as that.

Chapter Six

FOR THE REMAINDER of the afternoon Christopher made a noticeable effort to be less "obtrusive" and "demanding." Maggie tried to ignore him and, for the most part, it worked. But every once in a while she would look up and there he would be, lounging in a corner, perched on the edge of her desk, observing her every move with bright-eyed interest and listening to her lectures intently. It was disconcerting, to say the least. Occasionally she would see him start to ask a question or make a comment, then remember their bargain and restrain himself. Once, forgetting himself, he started to reach for a textbook. Maggie snatched it away in a panic and thus reduced a full-scale disaster to a few raised eyebrows from her students, who wondered what had made their usually happy-go-lucky instructor so edgy. Christopher responded with an apologetic shrug and went to stand behind one of the students, reading over her shoulder.

Maggie concentrated her efforts on getting through the day, nursing a fantasy that if she could only reach the safety and sanity of her apartment, everything would be all right. For a brief time it almost seemed that fantasy would come true.

As she left the campus a little before six o'clock, she was alone. She got into her car, fastened her seat belt and started the ignition, blissfully alone. She made a left turn out of the parking lot and headed north on Powell

Road, beginning to relax. At the intersection of Powell and Indian Springs, as she waited out a red light, Christopher said, "What a great lot of work must have gone into planning this traffic system! Who is responsible for it, do you know?"

Maggie stifled a groan and accelerated as the light turned green.

During the fifteen-minute drive to her house, Christopher calculated that approximately thirty-five percent of all drivers ignored the yellow caution light. In his opinion this was an unacceptable flaw in an otherwise extraordinarily efficient system. He asked endless questions about the workings of the internal combustion engine, but it turned out he knew more than Maggie did, as gasoline-powered engines had been something of a hobby of his during his life. He seemed irritated that no one had yet thought to convert to totally electronic vehicles, and he spent a great deal of time arguing that solar-generated electricity was a far better choice for power vehicles.

Maggie alternated between amazement at his confident grasp of modern, even ultramodern technology, and dismay over his relentless presence. Not even her car was safe from his invasion.

There was one close call. Christopher reached for the gearshift, obviously intending to discern its purpose, while she was traveling on a straightaway at forty-five miles an hour. Maggie screamed at him, and he moved away, favoring her with a slightly injured look as he pointed out, "You realize, of course, that human beings were never meant to travel at these speeds."

"We weren't meant to die at them, either," Maggie muttered. As soon as she had spoken she regretted her choice of words, but Christopher, who had just discovered the dashboard radio, hardly seemed to notice.

She pulled into her parking space with her nerves only slightly the worse for wear. As she slammed the car door she was vaguely aware of an airplane passing overhead, and instantaneously Christopher was beside her. *That* was unnerving.

"What is that?" he demanded, his head tilted toward the twilight sky.

"An airplane." She couldn't remember when the airplane was invented, but was sure it was not before 1899. She felt a little smug as she explained, "A flying machine. People travel in them."

He looked astounded. Then his expression changed, becoming more thoughtful, though still a little dubious. "A flying machine, you say. They haven't yet converted to electric-powered automobiles, but they've achieved powered heavier-than-air flight."

"We've also been to the moon and back," she informed him carelessly.

But his reaction to that information was disappointing. "I knew a gentleman who used to write fiction based on such possibilities," he answered dismissively. "But these airplanes . . ."

"We've been using them for decades." Maggie kept her voice low as she entered her building. There was no one in sight, but she didn't want to take any chances. "We fought two world wars with them. We have one now that flies from New York to London in two hours." She looked at him as she inserted her key into the lock. "We had airplanes in the fifties. Why don't you know about them?"

"I never saw one. I never saw much of anything except television."

Maggie opened the door, but Christopher, with a distracted expression on his face, passed directly through the wall. It gave Maggie a queasy feeling to watch him do that. She had to pause before entering the apartment herself, drawing a deep breath and bracing herself for whatever might lie ahead. How much more bizarre could this get? And how much more could she reasonably be expected to bear before gratefully giving way to insanity?

Christopher was standing just inside the door when she stepped in, causing her to start as she met him. He didn't notice. One finger was laid thoughtfully aside his mouth, and his eyes were alight with that familiar glint of curious excitement. "Is it possible for you to travel in one of these airplanes?" he demanded.

"Of course."

"Will you do it? Tomorrow?"

She tossed her purse on the sofa and stripped off her hat and jacket. "No."

"Why not?"

"It's expensive," she replied impatiently, "and I don't have anywhere to go."

"But you *have* done it before?"

"Of course."

"Imagine," he said softly. "Men flying through the sky at incredible speeds, breaking through the clouds, piercing the firmament . . . how I would dearly love to experience such as that!"

Watching him, Maggie felt the irritation that had bubbled and seethed within her all day fade away, replaced by a sort of gentle indulgence. How could one resent a person who was so unreservedly delighted by everything that crossed his path? How could she resist his curiosity?

She crossed the room and picked up a magazine, flipping through it until she came to an ad for a major airline. The page depicted in full color both the sleek exterior and the somewhat-exaggerated luxurious interior of their craft.

"Here. This is what an airplane looks like."

He took the magazine from her, and for the first time all day Maggie did not wonder what the transaction might look like to an uninvolved onlooker. Nor did she step quickly away when he came close. Except for a slight rise in temperature, which might have been her imagination, being near him was just like standing near any other man. *I'm getting too used to this,* she thought with a resigned shake of her head, and she left him to his magazine as she went into the kitchen

She poured herself the glass of wine she had never gotten around to having the night before, and when she returned to the living area, the magazine was open on the sofa. Christopher was nowhere in sight. And in the midst of her sigh of relief, Maggie suddenly realized that she wasn't relieved at all. She was disappointed. She *had* grown used to him. In a mere eight hours she had become so accustomed to finding him everywhere she looked, to anticipating him in every thought, to tolerating—no, enjoying—his constant questions, that now, instead of being glad to have her privacy back, she actually missed him. That was a startling realization and one she was not entirely sure she wanted to examine too closely.

Fortunately, she didn't have to. As she turned with a resigned lift of her shoulders to turn on the stereo Christopher said behind her, "I hope you don't mind. I was looking around your rooms." He stood at the doorway to her bedroom, gesturing behind him. "I didn't have much chance last night. There's so much to see and learn— It *is* like a gramophone," he exclaimed, coming forward as the button on the stereo engaged and music issued from a soft-rock station. "Another music machine, just like the one in your automobile."

Maggie scowled, totally forgetting her sentiment of a moment ago. "As a matter of fact, I *do* mind. You can't just go wandering around a person's bedroom and bathroom without permission—"

"Don't be absurd," he responded carelessly. "I'm not physical. What harm can I do? Besides, I didn't object when you went poking about my house."

There was little arguing with that logic, so Maggie responded shortly, "And it's not a gramophone. It's a radio. It also plays records and cassette tapes."

"And these knobs control it?" He experimented with the volume and station controls. "What are cassette tapes?" He looked up suddenly with a smile that was as sweet as it was sincere. "I'm sorry. Am I being demanding again?"

Maggie hesitated, then turned one corner of her lips upward. "You can't help it, I guess. And to tell the truth, when I couldn't find you a minute ago I kind of missed you—for just a minute."

"Rather like one misses a puppy who is constantly underfoot, I would imagine," he observed with such self-effacing honesty that Maggie couldn't help smiling.

"Something like that."

"Is that wine?" he inquired suddenly, and came toward her. "May I?"

Startled, Maggie held out the glass to him and he took it from her. He held it up so that the light glanced off the ruby liquid; he brought it to his face as though inhaling the aroma, his eyes closed in appreciation. "Domestic," he murmured after a moment. "Not very good quality, and barely aged, but after so long it is like nectar to me."

"You can smell it?" Maggie inquired, astonished. For the first time she realized that Christopher himself had no scent, another eerie reminder that he was not what he seemed.

"Scent is the most powerful stimulant known to man. Each odor triggers a dozen memories, and each memory has a hundred separate associations...." He opened his eyes and smiled, charmingly, playfully. "And I am, and have always been, an unabashed sensualist. Scent, taste, touch, color, music...they are the things life is made of, are they not?"

In a few simple words he had given her more to think about than an entire course on nuclear physics. She had barely begun to untangle that philosophy in her mind when he asked, "Do you smoke cigarettes?"

Maggie blinked at the change of subject. "No."

"A pity. I used to enjoy a cigarette now and then, and sometimes I long for the taste."

Maggie wondered in amazement if it were possible that an addiction could last beyond the grave. But then his face softened with reminiscence and he added, "I was in Turkey once and smoked the most delightful concoction from a water pipe. Quite intoxicating, really. It reminded me somewhat of opium, although I must say I was never much of an admirer of that particular palliative."

Maggie's eyes twinkled as she took her glass from him. "That concoction is illegal now," she informed him. "So, by the way, is opium."

"I shouldn't wonder."

He wandered across the room, admiring her furniture and the few pieces of photographic artwork, and he stopped before a curio cabinet that held her collection of pewter miniatures. He stood there examining it for so long that Maggie grew uncomfortable, and she took a sip of wine.

He picked up a figure of Merlin holding a crystal ball, and he half turned to her, his smile sly. "So, the lady scientist is a mystic at heart. I suspected as much."

Maggie was unreasonably defensive about her collection of dragons, wizards and fairy castles, mostly because she spent an embarrassing amount of money on it. She told herself that the little figurines were an investment, but she had never bothered to investigate the potential return. The truth was, she simply liked them.

"Don't drop that," she said sharply. "It's expensive."

He replaced the Merlin and took a figure of a baby dragon just emerging from its shell. The dragon's forelegs were curved over the edge of the shell to assist its climb out. Its tail was cocked at a jaunty angle, its ruby-chip eyes glinted with mischief. Christopher held the figure in the palm of his hand, running his forefinger along the pewter ridges of the dragon's spine, and he smiled.

"I like this one," he said. "He looks like a troublemaker."

Maggie came over to him, warming immediately to anyone who could appreciate her taste in dragons. "That's my favorite, too. I call him Elliot."

"Any particular reason?"

"It's from a children's story. I'm not very imaginative when it comes to naming dragons, I'm afraid."

"Come to think of it, he does look a bit like an Elliot."

Maggie giggled, and Christopher's eyes met hers, crinkled with a smile. The warmth of the shared moment stole through Maggie with a potency as rich as the wine, and for a timeless collection of heartbeats it was easy to forget that he wasn't real. More importantly, it didn't matter whether he was or not. No one else had ever understood her dragons. No one else had ever told her her eyes were the color of wildflowers. Maggie almost thought she could begin to like having him around.

The moment was shattered by the buzzing of the doorbell, abruptly bringing Maggie back to earth. Maggie looked in confusion toward the door, and Christopher, with a curious lift of his eyebrow, put the dragon back on the shelf.

"Hi, sweetheart." Larry brushed her lips with a kiss as she opened the door. "I come bearing contracts instead of flowers. I know I'm a little early, but I thought we could go over the fine print before dinner."

"Ah, the ubiquitous boyfriend," Christopher murmured, and Maggie cast a distracted glance at him as Larry shrugged off his overcoat.

"Dinner?" she repeated blankly.

Larry draped his coat over a bar stool and turned, an expression of pained tolerance on his face. "You forgot," he stated. "You were going to cook."

"I didn't forget," Maggie defended quickly, though, of course, she had. "I'm just running a little behind schedule, that's all."

Larry smiled, not in the least deceived, and stroked her cheek affectionately. "That's all right. Your helplessness is one of the things I love most about you. It makes me feel needed."

"Helpless!" Christopher scoffed. He was scowling as though he had been personally insulted. "You're about as helpless as Queen Victoria. Why do you let him talk to you like that?"

Maggie turned quickly toward the kitchen. "Have a seat. Do you want some wine?"

"Thanks." Larry sank to the sofa and opened his briefcase. "Do you have anything in the refrigerator, or do you want me to run out and get a couple of steaks?"

"Make him take you to a restaurant," Christopher advised, disgruntled.

Maggie hissed under her breath, "Stop it!" And to Larry she called, "How about an omelet?"

"Sounds fine."

Christopher stood a few feet away from Larry, his arms crossed and his brows knit thoughtfully as he studied the other man. Maggie hastily filled a wineglass for Larry, then topped off her own, trying not to think about what a disaster this could turn out to be. She had handled Christopher all day and in front of hundreds of students; she could make it through the evening.

"Do you find him attractive?" Christopher asked curiously.

Maggie took a gulp of wine, added more to her glass, and hurried to the living room. She did her best imitation of a relaxed smile as she handed a glass to Larry and sat beside him.

But, to her great annoyance, she found herself looking at Larry out of the corner of her eye and making observations she never would have bothered with before. She had always considered Larry a fairly good-looking man, even though appearances weren't top priority with Maggie by any means. He had a pleasant, if nondescript face, an open smile, a firm but gentle touch. He was well groomed, and he wasn't too tall. Of course, his sandy hair was beginning to thin a little on top, and he could have benefited by a couple of hours a week at the gym, but things like that weren't really important to Maggie. She never would have noticed if Christopher hadn't asked that ridiculous question.... If Christopher, with his dark, dynamic good looks hadn't been standing right next to very ordinary-looking Larry and making comparisons impossible to avoid.

Larry launched into an explanation of the contract, and Maggie did her best to pay attention. Christopher lost interest at once, and Maggie kept darting her eyes around, following him, holding her breath lest he do something to draw attention to himself. Mercifully, he kept his hands behind his back, pacing restlessly, casting more and more frequent dark glances toward Larry.

"Is this going to be a long evening?" he demanded after a time.

Yes, Maggie wanted to shout at him. *Yes, it's going to be a long evening, and the best thing for you to do is come back when it's over....*

"So you see," Larry was saying, "if the bank will go a thirty-year mortgage with a variable rate, I think you'll be much better off in the long run by investing your capital..."

"Good Lord," exclaimed Christopher in disgust. "The man is as dry as dust. This is what you call a courtship?"

"I agree," Maggie said firmly. To herself she thought, *I am being tested. That's it. This is all part of some grand design to prepare me for some higher destiny....*

Suddenly the radio blared out a hard-rock station at full volume. Larry jerked his head around, Maggie jumped to her feet, and Christopher declared, "What incredible music!"

"What in the world—"

"It's okay," Maggie shouted, climbing over Larry's feet as she rushed to the stereo. "The stereo's been on the blink...." She snapped the switch off, and it took all her willpower not to whirl furiously on Christopher. She smiled nervously at Larry and added into the silence, "Crazy thing. Must be a wire loose or something." Her heart was pounding.

Larry started to get up. "Want me to take a look at it?"

"No." Quickly, she came back over to him. "I hardly ever use it anyway. I'll take it into the shop when I get a chance."

Christopher shrugged and went over to the window.

"All right." Larry took both her hands and drew her down onto the sofa beside him, smiling. "Enough business for a while. Let me say a proper hello."

Larry's lips had barely brushed hers when Christopher turned with one eyebrow cocked in disapproval and interest. Maggie slid none-too-gracefully from Larry's embrace, reaching for her glass.

Larry's expression sharpened with concern. "What's wrong?"

"Nothing," Maggie assured him quickly, sipping her wine. This was not going to work. It definitely was not going to work. How could she be expected to have a normal life—to say nothing of a normal sex life—with a ghost looking over her shoulder every minute of the day? "I'm just a little on edge, I guess."

"Umm-hmm." Larry slipped an arm around her shoulders and drew her close. She tried not to resist. "And I know why. It's the house, isn't it?"

"Well..."

"And more than that." His tone was serious, and his fingers kneaded the back of her neck in what would have, at any other time, been a soothing, comforting motion. Tonight it only made her muscles knot.

"Honey," he said quietly, "I've been thinking about this a lot, and I want you to think about it, too. Buying a house is a big commitment, and you've admitted yourself you're not very good with commitments. I wonder if you weren't pushed into this one because I was pressuring you into another kind of commitment."

Christopher came over and listened with interest.

Maggie tried to laugh. It was a feeble sound. "Come on, Larry. Don't you think I'm capable of making independent decisions—with or without your input?"

His fingers stopped kneading her neck, and she realized how harsh her words had sounded. "I know you are. I just want you to be very sure this is what you want to do...and that you're not just doing it as a polite way of telling me to get lost."

Again she laughed, and again it wasn't very convincing. "If I wanted to tell you to get lost, I could find a less expensive way to do it."

"So could I," Christopher muttered, and Maggie tensed at the sound of his voice.

Larry smiled and brushed his fingers lightly through her hair. "I just want to take care of you. You know that, don't you?"

"You need taking care of less than any woman I've ever known," Christopher said impatiently. "Don't let him use that line on you. *He's* the one who needs taking care of."

Maggie's nerves were wound into such a fine knot that she could have screamed at the drop of a pin. She jumped up and said brightly, "You know what I want to do? Sign that contract and then go out to celebrate. Let's do that, okay?"

"You're not going to sign it without reading it?" Christopher protested as Maggie went in search of a pen.

Larry chuckled. "I should have known you'd find a way to get out of cooking. Here, I've got a pen right here."

Maggie turned to see Christopher bending over the contract on the coffee table. Larry was reaching for it at the same time. Maggie took a step forward as Christopher exclaimed, "You can't sign this!"

It all happened at once. Maggie rushed toward them, Larry reached for the contract, Christopher deliberately knocked Larry's wineglass over, spilling the liquid all over the papers. Maggie snatched up the sodden contract before Larry could even react, and something within her snapped. She cried furiously, "What did you do that for?"

Larry looked startled. "It was an accident. The glass must have been sitting on the contract."

"Do you have any idea of the price he's asking?" Christopher demanded. "You can't sign that!"

Maggie waved the dripping papers back and forth. "I know what I'm doing!"

"Hey, it's just paper," Larry insisted, rising. "There's no need to get upset. It can be retyped."

"I'm not sure you do," Christopher said. "If you were about to agree to something that foolish—"

"If you don't want me to have the house, just say so! There's no need to resort to childish tricks!"

Larry's face hardened, and that was when Maggie came to her senses. She had been yelling at Christopher; Christopher, who existed for no one but her; Christopher, who was standing behind Larry so that Larry received the full brunt of her wrath. Now hurt and insulted, Larry thought she was angry at him....

She couldn't believe she had done anything so foolish. She couldn't believe she had lost control like that. She took a single step forward, chagrined. "Larry, I'm sorry. I'm just not myself today."

He turned stiffly to pick up his briefcase. "Obviously not. I think I'll leave the contract with you. You should be able to dry it off and then if you want to sign, do. If not, let me know."

"Larry..."

He started for the door.

"Don't forget your coat," Christopher said.

Maggie hurried to the door and picked up Larry's coat. He looked at her for a moment, then took it from her.

"I'll call you," he said, and left.

Maggie leaned heavily against the door when he was gone, refusing to look at Christopher, trying her best to count to ten. She reached seven.

"How dare you!" she exploded. Her voice was low and shaking with barely suppressed emotion. "Who do you think you are? This is exactly the kind of thing I was talking about—"

"That shyster was about to bilk you out of thousands!" retorted Christopher. "You expected me to just stand by and let that happen?"

"He isn't a shyster, and he wasn't bilking me out of anything! I know exactly what the price is!"

"But that's absurd! The house cost me less than ten thousand to build, and even that was extravagant—"

"That was a hundred years ago!" she screamed at him. It felt good to let go. If she could have found something to throw, she would have done so and felt even better. "Things have changed since then! Money is different! Everything is different! You have no right to interfere in what you don't understand!"

To his credit, Christopher restrained hasty words, though the tight lines in his face did not relax and his eyes still churned. "Things can't have changed that much."

"You don't know the half of it!"

The high level of emotion was exhausting, and with those last words the worst of Maggie's anger burned itself out. She turned abruptly and began to separate the pages of the contract, spreading them out on the counter to dry. "It's a fair price," she said in a clipped tone. "More than fair. I want this house and I'm willing to pay for it. *What* I pay for it is none of your business. If you don't want me to have the house..."

She turned then and looked at him closely. A hollow feeling formed in her stomach, and she felt betrayed. If he didn't want her to have the house what could she do? He was a *part* of that house. How could she ever live there against his wishes?

She said hesitantly, a little breathlessly, "That's it, isn't it? You don't want me to have the house. But why? I've told you—"

"Of course, I want you to have the house." He made an impatient, dismissive gesture with his hand. "It's your house. Who else should I want living there—some stranger?"

And just as Maggie was about to release a breath of gratitude and relief, he went on, "Although I must say if I had any choice in the matter—" and he fixed her with a hard glare "—which I obviously don't, I'd go to some lengths to keep that slick-talking salesman of yours from ever setting foot in my home."

Now Maggie felt her ire begin to rise again. "What have you got against Larry?"

"He's a dolt," replied Christopher with feeling. "He hasn't got an iota of sense about architecture, and he has no taste whatsoever. He wants to cover my floors with nylon and replace stained glass with windowpanes. He can't tell oak from cypress and thinks age is a handicap instead of a commodity. The only thing that puzzles me is what *you* see in him. You strike me as a woman with better taste."

Maggie observed him in growing astonishment. "If I didn't know better, I'd say you were jealous."

"Only insofar as my house is concerned," he assured her forcefully.

"But what does Larry have to do with your house? He's only the agent. *I'm* the buyer."

"Well, naturally, when the two of you marry—"

"Marry!" She stared at him. "What makes you think I'm going to marry him?"

His expression sharpened. "Aren't you?"

"Of course not!"

In utter exasperation, she walked away from him, retrieving a sponge from the kitchen counter and beginning to mop up the spilled wine from the coffee table. A few drops had stained the carpet, and she did her best to blot it, muttering all the while over the damage he had done.

After a time Christopher spoke up. "If you don't intend to marry the salesman, why are you keeping company with him? And don't tell me your relationship is only business, because I saw you kiss him, several times."

"Oh, for heaven's sake!" Maggie scowled at the stain on the carpet, which she had somehow managed to make worse, and stalked into the kitchen to rinse out the sponge. "Just because a woman kisses a man doesn't mean she has to marry him—not in *this* century, anyway."

Christopher's eyes twinkled with a sudden change of mood that already Maggie had begun to think of as characteristic of him. "Fortunately," he agreed, "not in mine, either, or I should have been jailed for bigamy many times over. But you didn't answer my question. Why are you keeping company with him?"

Maggie squeezed out the sponge and placed it on the counter, turning to face him with her palms braced against the sink. Despite the provocation—and she had had plenty of it during the day—Maggie was discovering that maintaining a temper with Christopher was not easy to do. The questions he asked made her think, and she couldn't be angry and analytical at the same time.

"Because I like him," she answered. "He's a nice guy, and in this day and age nice guys aren't easy to find."

"He seems polite enough," Christopher agreed reluctantly.

"He's more than polite. I enjoy his company, and that's all you need to know."

"You could do much better than a mere salesman," Christopher asserted. "And at your stage in life you shouldn't be wasting your time on flirtations."

Maggie didn't know whether to be flattered at his implication that Larry was somehow not quite good enough for her or insulted by his reference to her "stage of life." "What *should* I be doing?"

"Getting married."

Maggie didn't know quite how to react until she remembered his nineteenth-century background, and then she was amused. "Why?"

"Because it's the natural order of things, that's why."

"You never married," she pointed out.

"It's different for a man."

"Not anymore it's not," she replied with a definite smirk of superiority, and Christopher's expression grew thoughtful.

"I'm not sure that's a good thing," he said slowly. "A woman wasn't meant to live alone. But then—" his smile seemed slightly wistful "—neither was a man."

Maggie wanted to pursue that, feeling for the first time as though she was on the verge of an insight into the man who once had been Christopher Durand. But he didn't give her a chance.

He said briskly, "I apologize for interfering in your personal life. I know it's not my place. I shan't promise it won't happen again, but I do apologize."

Maggie's lips tightened with a rueful smile. At least he was honest about it. But then his reference to the possibility of its happening again sank home, and she sobered.

"You're right," she said firmly, beginning to get a grasp on her former anger. "It isn't your place, and it *can't* happen again. I have my own life, don't you see that? There's no room for you in it! This isn't fair, and you just can't keep it up. You've got to go away."

He shook his head with a slow smile and regarded her patiently. "For such a bright young lady, you can be awfully dense about some subjects. Haven't you understood yet that it isn't my choice?"

He had made a similar reference earlier in the day, and it had made no more sense then than it did now. "Why not?" she demanded, frustrated. "You're the one with all the supernatural powers. You're the one who's breaking all the rules of physics—and metaphysics, too, for that matter! You can do what you want to."

"I don't have any supernatural powers," Christopher told her tolerantly, as though he were endeavoring to explain a particularly dull subject to a not-too-bright child. "My 'powers,' as you call them, are just as natural to me as yours are to you. And if I could do what I want to, I would be flying in one of your airplanes now, or attending the theater in London, or splitting an atom beneath the lens of one of those electron microscopes you were lecturing about—those would be *my* choices!"

Some of what he was saying was beginning to get through to her, but still it made no sense. "All right, then," she challenged him, "if you're not responsible, just who is?"

He gave her a peculiar look. "There seem to be only the two of us involved."

For a moment Maggie did not comprehend his meaning. Then she gasped. "Me? You're suggesting that I— But how can I have anything to do with this? I'm just an ordinary person. I'm not psychic or...or clairvoyant or anything, and if I had my way none of this would ever have happened! I just told you, I don't even *want* you here."

His smile was faint and abstracted. "Don't you?"

And before she could reply to that incredible suggestion, he clasped his hands behind him and walked a few steps away—a pose Maggie was beginning to recognize as indicative of secret excitement.

"I've given this some thought," he said, "and it seems perfectly clear to me. It's like..." He paused, searching for words, then turned. His eyes were bright and earnest. "It's like television. Signals are broadcast constantly, are they not? But they are meaningless—invisble, intangible, soundless—unless someone turns on a receiver. *You* are the receiver."

Maggie was stunned. It did sound simple when he said it. It made perfect sense. No one else could see him except her; he was invisible, soundless, intangible, to everyone except her. But even as the theory intrigued her, she rejected it.

"No," she said firmly. "If the receiver can be turned on, it can also be turned off. I should be able to make you go away if I want to, and I can't."

"Maybe you don't want to," he suggested.

"But I just told you—"

"Maggie, it's the only thing that makes sense," he insisted. His eyes were bright, and his tone was laced with quiet excitement. Maggie realized suddenly that the answer to the puzzle meant as much to him as it did to her, and it was that urgency that made her take him seriously.

"There's something about you that's different from everyone else," he said, "something that makes it possible for us to communicate, something that makes it impossible for you *not* to see me. It may be something even you don't recognize consciously, but on some level you do want me here, as much as I want to be here."

Maggie hesitated. The more he said, the more she was forced to recognize an underlying truth in his words. Consciously she did not want him here; so far his presence had been nothing but trouble, and it could only get worse. She did not need this kind of complication in her life, and God only knew she hadn't asked for it. But subconsciously...

"Curiosity?" she suggested softly.

Christopher gave a satisfied nod. "That's as good an explanation as any. You're a scientist faced with an unknown that has troubled mankind since the beginning of time, and your curiosity won't let you pass it by. There's a part of you that's enjoying this."

"A very small part," Maggie murmured. But her heart had picked up an increased rhythm, and she could not deny the chord of truth he had struck. Yes, she was curious. And captivated and charmed and delighted as often as she was irritated by Christopher. And if she had never met him, she would have missed the most exciting part of her life. Once in a million lifetimes something like this might happen; how could she wish it had *not* happened to her? And what was going to happen to her life now that it had?

"All right," she conceded reluctantly. "I'll admit that—just maybe—in some small way I'm...excited by all this. Glad, even. I mean, you are—interesting. I can't help being, well, fascinated by you."

His eyes danced with a sudden familiar mischief, and he made a small bow from the waist. "How relieved I am to know that, even after all these years, I haven't lost my effect upon the opposite sex."

No, thought Maggie, letting her eyes sweep once more in appreciative wonder over his lean figure. He hadn't lost that in the least.

"But," she added, somewhat more forcefully than was necessary, "that doesn't mean I have to like any of this. I'm a private person. I'm used to doing things my way, living alone, having time to myself. You can't keep interfering in everything I do, popping up every time I turn around...."

"I shall try to be discreet," he assured her gravely.

"Well...good." Maggie eyed him dubiously but didn't know what else to say. "As long as we understand each other."

"Of course."

He just stood there, looking at her with an expression of such assumed gravity she had to suspect that mischief was going on behind those bland eyes somewhere. She rubbed her hands together awkwardly and straightened her shoulders.

"Well," she said. "I'm going to take a bath and then make some dinner."

"All right."

He didn't move, so she walked past him. Halfway to the bedroom door she turned and, just as she suspected, he was watching her. "I'm going to take a bath now," she repeated, with slight emphasis on the last word.

"Yes." He smiled politely. "So you said."

"Well?" She gestured impatiently toward him. "Don't you think this would be a good time for you to be discreet?"

"I beg your pardon?"

Maggie felt her color rise, though whether it was from exasperation or embarrassment she couldn't be sure. "You don't expect me to take off my clothes with you here watching me, do you? Go away!"

He laughed. "You can't be serious! What difference can it make? I'm not physical, remember?"

"Maybe not," Maggie insisted irrationally. "But you're still a man, and young and—well, attractive."

He lifted his eyebrows, flattered. "Do you think so?"

Maggie scowled, her cheeks stinging hotter. "It doesn't matter what I think. The point is, if I can't be comfortable in my own home—"

"You're really being quite silly, you know," he pointed out gently.

Maggie knew he was right, and that fact embarrassed her as much as her uncalled-for display of modesty had done. Obviously, if she was going to live with a ghost she would have to learn to rise above social inhibitions and think as he did—especially since he left her no choice. After a moment she walked into the bedroom and closed the door.

She closed the bathroom door, too, and locked it for good measure. It was that gesture, and the futility of it, that finally put things into perspective, and she even chuckled out loud at her own foolishness. He wasn't a real man, after all. Being shy about undressing when he was around was about as enlightened as cowering before her own shadow. Besides, he wasn't around. He was probably in the living room, watching television or endeavoring to take her stereo apart.

Nonetheless, Maggie cast more than one furtive glance over her shoulder as she filled the tub with steamy water and tied her hair away from her face. By the time she had brushed her teeth and removed her makeup, she was beginning to relax.

She had undressed down to her jockey briefs and cotton T-shirt and was testing the water temperature with her toe when suddenly there was a delighted laugh behind her.

"You're wearing men's underwear!" Christopher exclaimed.

Maggie snatched up a towel and whirled, but he was nowhere in sight. A low chuckle seemed to be coming from the other side of the door.

"I never promised not to look," Christopher reminded her.

"You said you had outgrown your carnal impulses!" Maggie accused.

He was still chuckling. "I lied."

Maggie let out a growl of rage and threw the towel toward the door. It didn't hit anything, but it made her feel better.

Chapter Seven

MAGGIE PAUSED BEFORE the gold lettering that read Earth Visions and then, squaring her shoulders a little, pushed open the door. In contrast to the chill, drizzling day outside, the shop was an oasis of light and warmth. As the echo of the tinkling shop bell died away, she stood just inside the door, blinking a little in the brilliance.

The floors were covered in a soft turquoise carpet, the walls decorated with pastel portrayals of spirit guides, rainbows and otherworldly images Maggie could not begin to decipher. Brilliant white light bounced off glass display cases filled with semiprecious stones and avant-garde jewelry of every description: chunks of rose quartz, amethyst clusters and pale blue aquamarine; crystal pendants, ruby cabachons and fluorite wands. The shelves were lined with various colored candles and books on healing, self-awareness and crystal power. The entire shop was permeated with the faint but tantalizing odor of an exotic incense. Maggie thought, *Christopher would love this.*

Over the past week a tenuous truce had fallen over their relationship, and time had achieved what no amount of demanding or cajoling on Maggie's part could have done. As the exhilaration of discovery that characterized the first few days gradually wore off, Christopher's presence in her life became more of a permanent background fixture than a constant shock.

He no longer intruded into every waking moment, although his penchant for mischief would not allow him to resist surprising her when she most desired privacy. Oftentimes, she had discovered, he was present even when she couldn't see him, but she wasn't certain whether that was out of consideration for her or merely an energy-saving device on his part.

He attended her classes and listened quietly until he grew bored. Maggie was always a little insulted when he disappeared, until she remembered that even in the nineteenth century his grasp of mathematics and physics had far exceeded the junior-college level. There was not much she could teach him in that regard that he did not already know.

But his fascination with the computer, the VCR, the television and telephone was limitless, and Maggie was ceaselessly amazed by how quickly he absorbed the elements of modern technology and even began to expand on them. He reminded her of a starving man at a feast with his insatiable attraction to everything that was new and modern, and Maggie had to confess that the best moments of her life were spent watching him discover what she took for granted.

She no longer tried to deceive herself into thinking that she did not enjoy certain aspects of this supernatural phenomenon. But neither was she so far removed from reality that she could be entirely comfortable with it. There were times, late at night when she lay awake in the dark, when the old possibilities would start racing through her head again: Was she insane? Was she the unwitting victim of some dreadful biochemical experiment that was causing her to hallucinate this alternate perceptual state? Was she dreaming? Was she desperately ill and imagining all this?

Of course, when daylight overcame her paranoia, the doubts vanished and she had no difficulty accepting what was for her as real and as concrete as the earth beneath her feet. But neither could she ignore the fact that something was definitely wrong. She felt disoriented, isolated, trapped in secrecy.

Always before when life's problems had threatened, she had been able to seek refuge in her work, in the simple precision of mathematical equations and immutable laws. But her work offered no escape now because Christopher was always there, asking questions, making corrections, advancing theories. Even Larry, who in his own peculiar way had served as a sort of balance between the demands of her studies and the pressures of the outside world, was no comfort now. He had forgiven her readily enough for her inexplicable flare of bad temper when she brought him the signed, only slightly wine-stained contract. But the easy rapport that had always characterized their relationship had been impossible to reestablish with Christopher watching over her shoulder like a disapproving uncle. She had made excuses not to see Larry all week, and she was afraid his patience would soon run out.

But that was not the worst part. Maggie had never considered herself a particularly gregarious person until now, when she found herself inexplicably cut off from the rest of society by an extraordinary occurrence that she had neither sought nor wanted. That, by its very nature, demanded to be shared. She had to talk to someone. She had to find a way to put this in perspective and perhaps, in the process, even get an outside opinion. And she had to choose the person with whom she shared this exceptional information very carefully... Which was exactly what she was doing standing inside the Earth Visions crystal shop and bookstore, waiting for the owner to appear.

"Hello there, favorite person and bearer of the unlimited checkbook! Wait until you see what I've got for you."

Elena Barrett came through the door from the back with a flash of color and a tinkling of bangle bracelets, her arms extended and her eyes dancing with welcome. The two women embraced, and Maggie laughed, already beginning to feel better.

"I can't believe you'd just walk off and leave this place unguarded," she accused. "If I were a thief, I'd be in paradise."

"Not to worry. Your every move has been closely monitored and recorded for posterity on videotape. Where've you been lately? Let me look at you."

Elena stepped back, still holding Maggie's hands, and cast a critical eye over her friend's mismatched wardrobe. Maggie made a face. "Don't start with me. You're not going to sell me one of your overpriced rocks that's guaranteed to focus my energy and make me instantly beautiful. Believe me, I've got enough focused energy as it is."

Elena shook her head sadly. "When are you going to let me take you shopping? Just a few pieces, here and there, and you'd be surprised what you can do with yourself."

"I like myself the way I am, thank you very much," Maggie replied. She was amused, but she couldn't deny a small stab of envy for her friend's innate sense of style.

Before she opened her crystal shop Elena had been an image consultant, and the effects still showed. Her lustrous chestnut hair was so expertly cut that it fell into place with a shake of her head, her makeup so subtle and effective that it was almost impossible to tell where nature left off and cosmetic enhancement began. Her wardrobe was timeless yet always up-to-the-minute, in bold autumn colors that flattered her skin tone and figure. Her customers, expecting from the nature of the shop an exotic, even bohemian proprietress, were often surprised by the impeccably groomed, warmly businesslike woman who greeted them.

Maggie and Elena's unlikely friendship had begun two years before, when Maggie had wandered into the shop under the mistaken impression that jewelry repairs were done there. The broken clasp on her watch was forgotten in favor of a small pewter dragon, and she had been a regular customer ever since. She had met Larry, who knew Elena from her image-consulting days, at a party Elena had given. In the fast-paced, often highly competitive world in which Maggie lived, Elena was her closest woman friend, a confidante and playmate who was always ready with advice, philosophy or just plain silliness when Maggie needed it. She was the only person Maggie knew who would understand—or at least listen to—what she was going through now.

But it was so nice just to be here, to relax for a moment and forget everything she had left behind, that Maggie was in no particular hurry to bring the subject up. She demanded eagerly, "So what have you got for me?"

Elena gave her a conspiratorial wink and went behind the counter, bending down to retrieve a small box. "I didn't even put it out. I was afraid someone might buy it and you'd never forgive me. Of course, most of the purists are insulted by the lead crystal they use in these things, but as far as I'm concerned, who cares? Look."

As she spoke, Elena carefully unwrapped the layers of tissue paper and lifted out a pair of miniature dueling dragons. Each wielded a small, stone-studded sword, and one held victoriously a lead-crystal orb. Maggie caught her breath in delight when she saw them.

"Oh, yes!" she exclaimed. She held the pewter vignette in her cupped hands, grinning as she examined the fierce expressions on the combatants, tracing the exquisite craftsmanship with a wondering finger. *Christopher will love this,* she thought for the second time that day, and so enraptured was she with the discovery of the dragons that she didn't even notice the way Christopher had begun to insinuate himself into her most private thoughts.

"Wrap it up, put it on my charge card and don't even tell me how much it costs," Maggie said, surrendering the figures to Elena and opening her purse.

Elena chuckled as she took Maggie's card. "If I had a couple of more customers like you, I'd be a rich woman."

"You *are* a rich woman," Maggie corrected. "Only the very rich would have the nerve to charge seventy-five dollars for a rock you could dig up in your back yard."

"Bite your tongue, you're talking about my livelihood."

When the transaction was completed and Maggie had carefully tucked the box containing the dragons away in her purse, Elena went to the door and hung up the Closed sign. "You're just in time for lunch," she announced, "and I have half a tuna-salad croissant with your name on it. Come on in back and tell me everything that's been going on. Have you managed to spend your inheritance yet, or shall I order some more dragons?''

The back room was little more than an oversize storage closet, as drab and nondescript as the rest of the shop was charming. It was furnished with a sagging plaid sofa, a couple of canvas sling chairs, several packing crates and a coffee maker. Maggie always felt comfortable there.

"As a matter of fact," Maggie answered, pouring a cup of coffee, "I did manage to spend most of it—on a down payment for a house."

"You did it!" Elena exclaimed. "Good for you."

Maggie nodded, kicking off her shoes and curling her feet beneath her on the sofa. "We close in thirty days."

Elena who was dividing the tuna croissant with a plastic knife, suddenly stopped and struck out playfully at her. "You rat! I can't believe you kept a secret like this from me—and Larry didn't say a word, either. Don't I even get to look at the place? Since when do you go making a life-altering decision like this without consulting your best friend?"

Maggie smiled into her coffee. "Life altering" was right. "As a matter of fact, it was kind of an impulsive decision."

"Impulsive? You? It must be some house!" Elena transferred half the croissant to a napkin and pushed it across the packing crate toward Maggie. Her eyes were bright and eager. "So tell me," she insisted. "Every detail."

Maggie didn't see any point in putting it off. "For one thing," she said, "it's haunted."

Elena's eyes went wide; she had difficulty swallowing the bite of the sandwich she had just taken. "You're kidding!" she managed at last. "That's fantastic! How do you know? Cold spots? Noises? Was there some kind of gruesome murder there or an old Indian grave or what? Who told you it was haunted?''

Once again Maggie allowed herself the luxury of a small smile. Cold spots, Indian graves...if only it were that simple. "No one told me." She pinched off an edge of the sandwich and popped it into her mouth. "I saw the ghost."

The excitement in Elena's eyes turned to astonishment. She stopped with her sandwich halfway to her mouth. "You *saw* it! You, of all people?"

Maggie nodded.

"My God," Elena said softly. "You aren't kidding, are you? You really saw it?"

Again Maggie nodded.

"My God," Elena repeated, staring at Maggie. "I've never known anyone who's actually seen a ghost before—not anyone I could trust, anyway. This is incredible. A real ghost?" Her face became animated with excitement again. "So, what did you see? Was it just like a blob of something floating in the air or a full figure? Did it toss things around or speak to you or just stand there? *Tell* me!"

Elena's enthusiasm was encouraging, but her rather conservative understanding of all things paranormal made Maggie a little uncomfortable. She was almost tempted to make something up to appease Elena and then let the subject drop. But she had gone this far; no matter what happened, she would never forgive herself if she didn't tell the truth to at least one person. And Elena was the most open-minded person she knew. Elena had once had a boyfriend in Los Angeles who made his *living* talking to spirits, for heaven's sake.

Surely she wouldn't be shocked by anything Maggie had to say.

Maggie said cautiously, "I guess you'd call it a full-figure sighting."

"Male or female?"

"Male."

Elena leaned forward intently. "What did he look like?"

Maggie hesitated. "Well, you know those pictures of Lord Byron in all the literature books?"

"With those soulful dark eyes and the high shirt points and lace cravat?"

"Well, yes. Sort of like that. Except this one wears designer jeans and watches MTV."

For a moment Elena's expression didn't change. And then, abruptly her lips tightened in rueful annoyance, and she picked up her forgotten sandwich again. "Darn you, Maggie Castle, I should have known you were pulling my leg. That's not a bit funny, you know, and you really had me going, too. So—" she took a bite out of her sandwich "—tell me about your house."

Maggie tried to push back the first tight pangs of frustration. "I'm not kidding," she said. And when Elena only shrugged, she repeated firmly, "Elena, look at me: I am not kidding."

Elena looked at her and seemed to hesitate. A hint of doubt crossed her eyes and then was dismissed. "Come on, Maggie." She reached for the Diet Coke she had set on the floor. "MTV?"

"He's been dead a long time," Maggie said, and as much as she tried to prevent it, a note of frantic insistence was creeping into her voice. She hadn't realized just how important it was that Elena believe her until this minute, and now it seemed like the most important thing in the world that she convince her friend she was telling the truth. "He likes television and rock music because they're new to him, that's not so hard to understand! Just like he likes airplanes and electric blenders and driving a car—"

Elena almost choked on her Coke, though Maggie suspected it was more from amusement than amazement. "He drives a car?"

"No, he doesn't *drive* a car," Maggie explained impatiently, "he likes to watch me drive, and to talk about driving and look at engines..."

Elena, with the Coke can halfway to her lips, stopped and looked at her friend intently. She said, very carefully, "I half think you're serious."

"I *am* serious!"

With that same cautious, hesitant look on her face, Elena warned, "I swear to you, if this turns out to be a joke..."

"It's not a joke." Maggie did her best to sound calm, reasonable and not in the least bit desperate. "Have you ever known me to play this kind of joke?"

"No," Elena agreed thoughtfully. "I've never known you to play any kind of joke. I've always said you were the nicest uptight person I know, and if only you'd learn to relax and have a little fun..."

Elena stopped and frowned, as though impatient with her own digression, and then demanded helplessly, "Then what in the world are you *talking* about?"

Maggie took a deep breath. She tried to start at the beginning. "My house," she said, "the one I just bought, it was built by a man named Christopher Durand, who died in 1899. Only he didn't really die—he's just been kind of hanging around the house all this time."

"Watching MTV," supplied Elena dryly.

"Of course not." Maggie's voice was taking on an edge she tried hard to suppress. "There's no television in that house. The house is empty. That's why he's not at the house anymore. He's at my apartment . . . and in my classroom . . . and at the grocery store . . . just about everywhere. . . ." Maggie let her voice trail off, hearing with her own ears how outrageous the words sounded. She looked at Elena miserably.

Elena glanced at the half-eaten sandwich in her hand as though it had suddenly turned sour. Carefully she put both the sandwich and the Coke on the packing crate. She wiped her fingers with a paper napkin, then gently smoothed down the crisp pinch-pleats in her gabardine skirt. There was tenderness and reluctance in her eyes as she looked at Maggie.

"Maggie, I want you to understand that what I'm about to say is only because I love you . . ."

Helplessly, Maggie dropped her head back against the sofa cushions. "I am not losing my mind!"

"Listen to me. You've been under a lot of stress lately—"

"Elena—"

"What with your favorite aunt dying and coming into money suddenly and then buying a house when you *know* you've never lived in one place for more than two years at a time—"

"That has nothing to do with anything—"

"And here you are, teaching full-time and trying to complete your doctoral work in *physics*, for heaven's sake—Lord knows that's not easy—and then there's Larry pestering you like a damn fool to have his baby or something when you've worked all these years to have a career—"

"Will you ease up, already?" Maggie exclaimed in exasperation, sitting up straight and running her hands through her crushed curls. "I am not having a nervous breakdown, although if I sit here and listen to you much longer you just might talk me into one. I know what I saw!"

Elena's expression was at once both sympathetic and apologetic. "All I'm saying is no one would blame you for cracking under the strain. And if you'll only think about it a minute, it makes perfect sense...."

"Look, I'm sorry." Maggie reached for her shoes, suddenly realizing how foolish she had been to come here and expect Elena to buy a wild tale like the one she had just told. Maggie wouldn't have believed it if the positions had been reversed. If she didn't leave soon, she was in danger of losing both Elena's respect and her friendship, and the way things were going she needed all the friends she could get. "This was a mistake, so forget it. I just thought, of all the people I knew you might at least listen to me..."

"Maggie, wait." Elena laid a restraining hand on her arm, looking helpless and confused. "I'm sorry. I should know that you wouldn't make up something like this. It's just that it's so crazy—" She cut herself off abruptly. "Strike that. Poor choice of words. Listen, I want to believe you, I really do. Let's just start over, okay?"

Maggie hesitated. She desperately wanted—no, needed—someone to share this with, as though by doing so some of her burden could be diminished. But she realized slowly that no one could share it unless that person also experienced it; no one could truly understand without being in her shoes. It was beginning to look as though she was fated to work this thing out on her own. Still, she had to try.

Slowly she settled down on the sofa again. "I don't know how to make it sound any less outrageous than it is," she confessed.

Elena nodded, her perfectly sculpted eyebrows drawn together thoughtfully. "Then let's just take it one step at a time. You say he talks to you?"

"As clearly as you're talking to me now."

"What does he talk about?"

"Everything. The weather, the news, quantum physics, what I'm having for dinner...he has an opinion on everything."

"You make him sound so—" Elena swallowed, as though she were having trouble with the words "—real."

"He *is* real," Maggie explained earnestly. "Real and three dimensional, not like those shadowy spectral things you see on television horror shows.... If you passed him on the street, you wouldn't look twice. He's just like an ordinary person, except that he can walk through walls and disappear and no one can see him except me."

Maggie could see the struggle in her friend's eyes, and she had to admire her self-control, if nothing else. At last Elena said softly, "Wow!" and sank back in her chair, as though exhausted by the effort of keeping her incredulity to herself. For a moment neither woman spoke.

Then, choosing her words carefully, Elena said, "I don't know how much you know about the spirit world, and Lord knows I'm no expert, but what you're saying...it just doesn't make sense, do you know what I mean?"

Maggie nodded glumly, and Elena, encouraged, went on, "I mean, maybe there are spirit guides and poltergeists and haunted houses—I mean, people at the White House *still* say they see Abraham Lincoln walking around—and maybe there's some truth to those stories about the long-dead relative who came to sit on the edge of the bed and warn people about a disaster.... But *this*. I never heard of anything like this."

"Me, either," agreed Maggie. Deep inside, a small kernel of hope began to flower because at least Elena appeared to be taking her seriously. "And I don't even believe in poltergeists or spirit guides."

"Unless..." Elena's expression grew darker and more troubled as she examined an unspoken possibility in her head. When she looked at Maggie again it was with new resolve. "Maybe what you need is professional help."

With a sharp breath of undisguised exasperation, Maggie reached for her purse.

"No, for heaven's sake, I didn't mean *psychiatric* help."

Maggie looked at her friend warily.

"Although I can't say that I'm absolutely, one-hundred-percent convinced about everything you've said," Elena had to add honestly, "I believe *you* believe it. And you're not the kind of person to make up something like that from whole cloth, so there's got to be some kernel of truth there...."

"Thanks," Maggie said dryly. "At least we're getting somewhere."

Elena looked defensive. "I am trying to help, Maggie."

"All right, I know you are." But Maggie felt more impatient than chagrined as she added, "What's your suggestion?"

"What I was about to say," continued Elena staunchly, "is that maybe what you have here is an earthbound spirit. And if that's the case, you're not qualified to deal with it. You should bring in a professional."

Maggie's curiosity was piqued. "What do you mean, 'earthbound'?"

"Well, like I say, I'm no expert," Elena explained, obviously on easier ground now, "but from what I understand, the natural order of things is for souls who have passed over, so to speak, to continue on their journey to a higher destiny, whatever that might be. But sometimes they get trapped. They can't go forward and they can't go back. It's really a tragic thing."

Maggie was unwillingly intrigued. "What would cause something like that?"

"Any number of things. Maybe some trauma in their previous life, like a violent death or an injustice of some sort, even an unrequited love. Most of the time it has to do with something they left unfinished on earth, something they feel compelled to complete before they move on. In any case, it seems that these are desperately unhappy souls who are doomed to wander the earth until someone sets them free."

"Like an exorcist?"

Elena grimaced a little. "That sounds so Hollywood, doesn't it?"

"It sure does." Maggie simply could not picture herself going to those lengths. The very thought caused her to suppress a shudder of dread.

But Elena had given her a lot to think about. Perhaps it had been a mistake to blurt her story out the way she had, and Maggie still wasn't sure how much of it Elena believed. But she couldn't regret coming here—

not entirely. She felt as though she had the beginnings of a tenuous, fumbling grasp on a situation that, before today, had completely overwhelmed her. She had a great deal of examining and sorting out to do in her mind, and she needed to be alone.

"Listen." Maggie tried to keep the worry out of her voice as she hooked the strap of her purse over her shoulder and prepared to rise. "You won't mention this to anyone, will you? I mean, it was hard enough for me to tell you, and I do have a reputation to think about—"

Elena lifted both hands as though in defense. "You know me better than that."

Maggie smiled. "Of course, I do."

But Elena's eyes were concerned as she stood. "If there's anything I can do..."

Maggie brushed her cheek with a kiss. "You've been great, really. Thanks."

"Call me," Elena insisted.

Maggie waved an affirmative as she made her way out the door.

Chapter Eight

ALL THE WAY HOME Maggie was distracted, thinking over what Elena had said. She did not need an expert in psychic phenomena to tell her that what was going on was unnatural. Disembodied spirits traditionally belonged to a higher realm, living humans occupied space on earth, and, under normal circumstances, never the twain should meet. Maggie had simply never realized *how* unnatural her situation was. Nor had she thought about it in explicit terms of right and wrong before. Earthbound spirits, tied to the physical plane by a trauma, waiting for something or someone to free them . . . it made a kooky sort of sense.

Christopher himself had as much as admitted that he was unable to leave. And there was certainly no doubt that he was bound to the trappings of the physical world—sight, sound, sensation—as surely as was any living being who walked the planet. But traumatized? Desperately unhappy? That was when Elena's theory began to fall apart. Maggie had never met a less desperately unhappy soul in her life, and if Christopher Durand had undergone any sort of trauma in his entire century-and-a-quarter of existence, he showed no signs of it now.

But still it bothered her, just as it had on a less clearly defined level from the moment Christopher appeared in her life. There must be some explanation. Something had gone wrong somewhere in the grand scheme of life and death, and for Christopher's sake and her own, Maggie had to try to set it right. Every equation had a solution. All Maggie had to do was find it, and Christopher would be freed from his earthly entrapment. It sounded very grand and noble.

The only trouble was, Maggie was not at all sure Christopher wanted to be free. And then Maggie had to ask herself a very disturbing question: All things considered, how badly did *she* want to be free of him?

She had barely begun to explore the possibilities inherent in Christopher's existence. There were so many subjects they hadn't discussed yet, so many universal puzzles to which he might hold the key. Wasn't the minor inconvenience afforded by this relatively harmless haunting worth the scientific knowledge she might gain?

On the other hand, did she have any right to keep him here by virtue of her curiosity? Wasn't it her moral duty to at least try to put to rights whatever had gone wrong in the process that had condemned Christopher to haunt the earth forever?

Of course, it was all sheer speculation, and Maggie was not accustomed to dealing with such weighty issues. She was not a philosopher, she had never had much interest in such things, and it was obvious she was out of her league. She wished she could just forget the whole thing.

Nonetheless, she was still turning the problem over in her head as she reached the door of her apartment and began the ritual search for her keys. They weren't in her purse. She patted the pockets of her coat. Not there, either. Frowning, she thrust her hands into her skirt pockets and came up with two pennies and a sales slip, but no keys. She opened her purse again.

"You locked them in your car." Christopher dangled her keys before her.

"Oh. Thank you." Maggie took them from him quickly before some innocent passerby could notice a set of keys hanging in midair. "I guess there are some advantages to having a ghost around, after all."

But Christopher didn't reply, and when she opened the door he was already inside, leaning against the bar. "I wish you wouldn't do that," Maggie complained. "It makes me nervous. Why can't you use doors like ordinary people?"

His eyes twinkled. "There's an obvious answer to that, you know."

After a moment Maggie's lips tightened in reluctant amusement. "Right." One thing had to be said for Christopher. No matter how foul her mood, no matter how great her irritation or deep her concentration, he could always eventually make her smile. And it was impossible to stay cross with him when his charm wrapped itself around her like a soothing mist.

He was wearing a cocoa-brown velour warmup suit and Nikes without socks, adapting himself easily to the casual attire of the after-work crowd he no doubt had observed around the apartment building. The outfit was particularly flattering to a man of his coloring and build, shaping the form of lean thigh muscles and tight calves beneath soft material, deepening the color of his eyes. More than anything else about him, Maggie was fascinated by his body—or rather, the way he presented himself. She could see the light dusting of hair on his forearms beneath the pushed-up sleeves of his shirt, and the tendons of his ankles where the pants ended in knit cuffs. Had he been this strong, this vital and attractive in real life? Or had he adapted this form out of vanity or some desire to please her?

Questions like that would eventually drive Maggie crazy. She took off her coat and tossed it on the chair, shaking the dampness of the foggy day from her hair. Christopher said, "Aren't you going to show me the dragons?"

Maggie turned to him, half in amusement, half in accusation. "You *were* there!"

He merely smiled. "May I see them?"

Maggie took the dragons from her purse and unwrapped them, but she couldn't help being a little disturbed. If Christopher had been at the shop with her the whole time, he had heard her conversation with Elena. What would he make of it? She almost preferred the distraction of being able to see him everywhere she went to the uncertainty of not knowing where he was.

She held out the dragons for him, and his pleasure, as it always did, melted away her lingering gloom the way sunshine dispersed fog on a gray day. He held them in his hands, exclaiming softly over the workmanship and the whimsy. "I shall call this one Pendrake," he announced, indicating the dragon on the lower level. "And this one—" he touched the dragon who held the crystal ball aloft "—is Ulyssia."

"A female?" Maggie inquired, surprised.

"Of course. The female is always victorious sooner or later, and as you can see, she has already claimed her prize." He held the figurine up so that the lead crystal prism caught the light and flung a rainbow of color on the ceiling. "What do you suppose the orb represents?"

"Truth," suggested Maggie, "power, beauty, justice..."

"Or love," he added, smiling to himself as he admired the dragons. "The most elusive prize of all."

The moment between them was as gentle as a watercolor painting, warmed by the lamplight, softened at the edges. The cold mist pressed at the windowpanes and life in all its busy mundanity went on outside the walls, but inside Maggie was secure and content. Simple pleasures, quiet moments . . . why couldn't it always be like this? Why couldn't it be real?

"I can see you breathing," she said softly, and brought her eyes to his in wonder. "How can I do that?"

"Perhaps because that is what you expect to see." Christopher turned and put the dragons on the shelf, carefully arranging a place of prominence for them between a wizard in flowing robes and a castle with a moat. "The mind is a remarkable tool, capable of making familiar patterns out of the thousands of pieces of nonsense it receives every day."

Of course. Maggie knew that. But his nonchalant, relentlessly intellectual attitude toward his own state was rather deflating, taking the edge off the sense of magic she always felt in his presence. She was annoyed with herself for finding that depressing.

Maggie went into the kitchen and opened the refrigerator door. She wasn't really hungry, but Christopher insisted that she have at least one hot meal a day. She had discovered it was easier to cook than to put up with his badgering.

"I hope you're not going to use that automatic cooker again." Christopher sat on a bar stool, watching her. "I'm not convinced food prepared that way is at all good for you."

"You mean it just doesn't smell as good when it's cooking." At first Christopher had been fascinated by the microwave, but had lost interest when he discovered the aromas generally inherent in food preparation were missing.

"Precisely. As any gourmand will tell you, half the enjoyment of a well-prepared dish, like that of a good wine, is in its bouquet. All of the senses should be involved in any worthwhile experience, not just one."

Maggie selected a baking potato and went over to the sink. "I could eat this raw and it would still supply the same nutrition," she pointed out. "Probably more."

"A very uncivilized attitude. Our ability to appreciate the pleasures of the flesh is what separates man from beasts, you know."

"Most people," Maggie replied dryly as she scrubbed the potato under running water, "would say it's the ability to think that separates us from lower species."

"Take it from one who has spent decades doing nothing but thinking," Christopher answered. "The intellect is highly overrated."

And there it was, the subject she had been unconsciously trying to avoid but which Christopher, either through accident or design, had left open to her. Maggie pricked the potato with a fork, her eyes on her work, and inquired nonchalantly, "Is that what it's like then, when a person—" she managed to hesitate only slightly over the word "—dies?"

She could feel his gaze on her, and she thought he wouldn't answer. She almost hoped that he wouldn't. But Christopher's curiosity was at least as great as her own; naturally he would understand the motives behind the question and answer it if he could—just as she would have done in his place.

"I can only answer for myself, of course," he replied after a moment. "It's...dull." His tone was thoughtful, as though he were traveling back through time, searching for memories. "Colorless. Like being trapped at the bottom of a murky stream. One can see, but not touch. Want, but not have. Imagine but not act upon those imaginings. Eventually there is nothing left to do but live inside one's own thoughts. It's not a state I would recommend highly."

An instinctive, primal chill went down Maggie's spine. She looked at Christopher, and his expression was steady and unapologetic, reminding her that she had, after all, asked. She wished she had not.

But now she understood, as she never had before, his unmitigated delight in all the things of her everyday life. How could anyone, corporeal or incorporeal, willingly choose the state he had just described over what he now had?

She put the potato in the microwave and set the timer. The oven engaged in a soft purr, and she turned back to Christopher. "And that's why you came back," she said. "Because you were bored."

He smiled. "You imply that I've been away, which of course I haven't. But, yes, indeed, boredom was a large part of my former existence. Boredom and..." A hint of puzzlement creased his forehead, as though he were surprised by the thought that had occurred to him. "Waiting."

"Waiting for what?"

He looked at her, and his eyes still reflected bewilderment. "I'm not sure." Then he shrugged and added lightly, "You, I suppose."

"That doesn't make any sense."

"Perhaps it's not supposed to. Not everything in life—" he grinned "—or elsewhere does."

But Maggie wasn't ready to accept that, not yet. There were always answers. And even though now she was a little afraid of what those answers might be, she had to at least try to find them.

She took a breath. "You heard what I was talking about with Elena this afternoon."

"Yes." His expression sobered. "I never realized how lonely it must be for you," he said gently, "being burdened by this secret. I know something of loneliness, and I never meant to bring it to you. I'm sorry."

Maggie was touched. It was in moments like this, when his natural propensity for playfulness was set aside for genuine emotion, that it became impossible to think of him as other than a real and living being. A being with the strengths and weaknesses, foibles and needs of any other human on earth. At moments like this, she *wanted* him to be real.

And now, of all times, she could not afford to forget that he was not.

She squared her shoulders and forced herself to say firmly, "You know that your being here like this isn't right. There's got to be a reason for it."

He shrugged elegantly. "I know nothing of the sort. I'm here because I want to be. There's nothing complicated about that."

She shook her head adamantly. "There's got to be more to it than that. Something you've left incomplete, some wrong you have to right . . ."

He chuckled, and the frank amusement that danced in his eyes made Maggie realize how simplistic Elena's theory was. "I had an exquisitely happy and fulfilling life," he assured her. "I traveled the world, I communed with the most learned men of the day, I designed and built with my own hands monuments that would outlast my memory. I knew the taste of a good wine and the feel of silk against my skin. I loved my share of beautiful women. What more could any man ask of life than that? If I have any regrets, it is only that I did not appreciate it more at the time."

His reply, though Maggie had no doubt that it was the unadulterated truth as he knew it, was frustrating to say the least. "There's got to be more to it than that," she insisted. Then she demanded abruptly, "How did you die?"

"Ah, that." He took on a pensive air. "The most tragic thing, really. I was in Egypt, uncovering the tomb of an ancient pharaoh. After three weeks, we reached an inner chamber and discovered a plaque which, when translated, promised death by tooth and claw to any who violated the sacred resting place. Well, naturally, we dismissed it as nonsense, but the native workers, being superstitious by nature, began to spread panic high and low. As a number of accidents plagued the site and the natives began abandoning us, we were forced to return to Cairo to procure more workmen. At our second night's camp we were suddenly attacked by a big cat—Bengal, as I could make out, a relentless creature straight from hell. One by one I saw my companions go down. I held the beast off as long as I could, but when I ran out of ammunition, I, too, fell victim to the curse of the tooth and claw."

For a while there, caught up in the spell of an expert storyteller, Maggie had almost been taken in. She regarded him steadily and pointed out, "There are no tigers in Egypt."

"Oh?" He feigned surprise, but his eyes were twinkling madly. "I must be thinking of something else."

The timer on the microwave chimed, and Maggie jerked open the door. "You're not being the least bit helpful."

"Be careful of your—"

In her frustration, Maggie tried to remove the hot potato without an oven mitt, and Christopher finished blandly, "Fingers," as she dropped the potato on the counter, shaking her scalded hand.

She scowled at him. "You could at least *try*."

She could see he was trying not to laugh. "Dear heart, I'm sorry, but I don't know what you want from me. Better run some cold water over your hand or you'll have a nasty blister."

Maggie's stomach gave a little flutter at his easy and no doubt unconscious use of the endearment, and she was irritated with herself for the reaction. No one had ever called her "dear heart" before. Why did the words make her feel so inexplicably lonely?

Her eyes suddenly stung with tears, and she blamed it on her burned fingers or perhaps her mounting frustration. She stalked to the sink and jerked on the faucet with unnecessary force, holding her hand under the cool stream of water. "We're not talking about what I want," she said shortly. "It has nothing to do with what *I* want. All I want to know is what *you* want. That's the whole point, isn't it?"

Her voice had started to rise with the last, and to her mortification, her tears, instead of fading as the pain in her fingers did, actually burned hotter, until one of them spilled over and splashed onto her cheek.

"What do I want?" Christopher was beside her. His voice was low and angry, and his entire form was tight with an even deeper emotion she did not understand. "Shall I tell you what I want, Maggie Castle of the endless equations and flawless solutions?"

Maggie caught her breath at his unexpected display and looked up at him through a shocked blur of tears. His eyes were dark and churning, and everything about him radiated tension and distress. "I *want*..." He thrust his hand beneath the running water. The stream flowed steadily, appearing to pass through his solid flesh, and Maggie shrank back a little. "To be able to feel this. And this." He grasped the faucet with his hand and twisted it viciously, turning off the water. "It should be cold, and smooth and solid, but to me it feels like air."

"Don't you understand?" he demanded of her, and his barely restrained emotion was like an electrical storm snapping in the air around her—contained, volatile, yet wild with kinetic energy. "Scents are only a memory to me, sounds a mere echo, even sights are only a composite of what I *wish* them to be. Your world is no more real to me than I am to you, and I want it to be different! Until there was you, I wanted nothing, and now I want everything. And nothing you or I can do can change that or make it easier or even explain it."

He stopped, and Maggie imagined she could hear his sharp intake of breath. She did not imagine the frustration she saw in his face nor the pain of helplessness as he brought his gaze back to her. "I want," he said simply, "to dry your tears, but I can't even do that."

"Oh, Christopher." It was barely a whisper, choked and miserable. If ever she had needed to be comforted or to give comfort, it was then. A touch, a gentle embrace, a clasp of the hand to bridge the need that yawned between them, to reassure and soothe the turmoil into which each of them separately and together, had been cast through no will of their own.... She ached with her own inadequacy and his pain, yet there was nothing she could do. Nothing.

"I'm sorry. For all the questions and—and stupid theories..." Gracelessly, she wiped her damp face with her sleeve and tried to swallow back the thickness in her throat. "It's just that I'm used to dealing with things that are a little more concrete, and ... I guess I have a one-way approach to problem solving, and ..."

She looked at him, and all her helplessness was reflected in her eyes. It did not occur to her to try to keep a secret from Christopher, although the words were hard to say. "Sometimes I wish you were real, too," she whispered.

His expression gentled with tenderness, softened with understanding. His smile was sad and sweet and it touched her like a caress. "I know," he said simply.

And there, again, was the moment of silent understanding and shared emotion, like others they had known before. Wrapped together and sealed apart from the rest of the world by their own secret communication, there was comfort in the simple act of looking at each other and knowing that neither of them was completely alone. But this time the moment was too intense, too full of uncertain yearnings and half-formed needs to be maintained for long. Maggie broke the eye contact first and drew in a shaky breath.

"I guess..." She cast her eyes about the room and tried to smile. "I guess that's one handicap of the modern age." She made a weak gesture with her hand. "Everything is too easy. I expect this to be easy, too."

"No." He smiled, too, though it was slow and rather vague. "The dilemma in which we find ourselves isn't easy. But perhaps it's not as complicated as it seems, either. You may have just given yourself the answer.''

She looked at him curiously.

"The modern age," he explained. "I've always felt I was born out of time, and I recall how eagerly I was looking forward to seeing the twentieth century. I was cheated of that, and perhaps that's the thing that's kept me around all these years. I merely wanted to see how it turned out."

"Yes," Maggie breathed, and allowed herself a cautious hope. "That could be it, couldn't it?"

His expression relaxed into a more genuine smile as he saw the expression on her face. "I would say it's as good an explanation as any."

"Of course. It makes perfect sense." And she could have laughed out loud with relief. Perhaps this wasn't the answer. Perhaps it was only part of it, but it was a straw to grasp in the whirling torrent of confusion, and Maggie was grateful for that. If Christopher was willing to accept the explanation, Maggie was willing to put her curiosity aside. Though deep inside a little voice warned her this was only a stopgap, that there was another, truer answer waiting to be discovered, Maggie refused to explore the mystery any further. Perhaps some things simply weren't meant to be explained.

And when she realized that she, who had never settled for half measures in her life, was actually allowing the mystery of the ages to pass by unnoticed, she did laugh out loud.

Christopher's eyes crinkled in appreciation. "And if it makes you that happy, then the matter is settled. I like to hear you laugh, Maggie."

Maggie felt warm all over. "I was just thinking about something Elena said, about my needing to loosen up.

Maybe I am, a little, after all. And wouldn't she be surprised to know that you're the reason?"

"Am I?" He seemed pleased. "Well, now, that's a noble enough reason to call anyone back from the grave. What are you going to do with that potato?"

Maggie chuckled again, amazed at how easy everything was with Christopher. They went from high emotion to mundanities, from despair to laughter in minutes and with no strain whatsoever. Had anyone ever challenged her so, made her feel so natural and open and right...so alive? How was it possible that he could be so wonderful, so infuriating, so appealing and exciting and tender and thoughtful and—so unreal?

"I am going to stuff it with broccoli and cheese and eat it," Maggie replied, taking a package of frozen broccoli from the freezer. "A bland dish for a man of your sophisticated palate, I realize, but it's nutritious."

"There's that word again," he complained. "Nutrition. It seems to be an obsession with your generation."

"Among other things." In the process of opening the package, she suddenly stopped and looked at him. "Christopher...what you said a minute ago." She did not want to bring back unpleasant memories, but she had to know. "You really can't...feel anything?" she ventured hesitantly. "Or taste...Because the way you talked about colors and smells and music, enjoying them so, I always thought..."

A brief shadow crossed his face. "I do enjoy being near them," he said, "but I can't really experience them, not the way you do. The music doesn't thrum through my blood, as it would yours, the scents only entice me to know them, and the colors, though vivid and beautiful, are nonetheless flat, one-dimensional, because they can't be touched. After so many years of missing them, even the hint of these things is an enormous pleasure to me... but it's not the same. It is the nature of all men, I think—" and he smiled a little "—not just departed ones, to yearn for what they can't have."

Maggie put the package aside. She did not even know what she was going to say until she spoke, but excitement was building like a small, curious tickle in the back of her throat. She said, "What would happen if I touched you?"

An alert look, one of surprise and interest, came into his eyes. "Why... I don't know."

Maggie took a step toward him and slowly he raised his hand, palm up, facing her. Maggie's heart began to pound. Dread and excitement coiled in her stomach, and she could not believe that she was doing this, that she wanted to do it, that she had ever suggested it.

Christopher's eyes were gentle and expectant, quietly waiting. His upraised hand was slim and gracefully formed, with long tapered fingers and skin that looked soft and warm. But what would it *feel* like to touch? Would it be cold and lifeless, as dead as stone? Would it feel like anything at all? Could she conceal her horror from him if her hand passed through his flesh and bone like a knife slicing through butter? If his image dissolved before her eyes, would she ever be able to believe in him again? She did not want to do this. But she had to.

Her heart was roaring in her ears now, and her breath was coming shallowly. Christopher's eyes beckoned her, steady and reassuring. She lifted her hand, and it was trembling. Slowly she brought it close to Christopher's, and then palm to palm.

There was an explosion of blue-white light, rushing warmth, dizzying, electrifying sensations. She forgot to breathe, she no longer felt her heart beat; indeed, she hardly was aware of her body except as it related to the flashing, pulsing, magnetic bombardment of sensation...a kaleidoscope of colors, a high, rich rushing sound in her ears, the taste of something achingly sweet on her tongue, and Christopher.... He permeated her, washed through her with light and liquid heat, charging electrons, magnetizing protons, rearranging atoms until she was not only touching him but, for a brief, elusive instant, she was a *part* of him. She was inside his thoughts as he was inside hers, and she knew, she tasted, she felt, she became a part of everything he had ever known or been. Exquisite joy, rending sorrow, loneliness, yearning, celebration, wonder, explosive elation and quiet bliss...they were hers, and they were his, and there was no seam at the joining. They were river and stream, flowing into one.

And then, abruptly, it was over.

Christopher stepped back, looking at his hand. Maggie could not move. Every nerve in her body was tingling; her limbs were strange, rubbery appendages whose function she could not, for a moment, recall. She gradually realized that the hissing sound she heard was her own thin breath, and she was dizzy, disoriented, yet filled with a pleasure and a wonder so intense she could hardly contain it; she thought it must radiate from her like heat waves that would soon ignite the room.

Christopher stared at his hand, slowly turning it over and back again, examining it. His expression was as stricken with amazement as hers was, and he whispered, "My God."

He looked at her. His eyes were dark with awe, alight with the memory of a miracle for which there were no words. But Maggie knew it; she shared it. She brought her hand to her throat as though to soothe the ache of a thousand things that needed to be said, but she could not speak. Nothing in her life would ever be the same after tonight. Nothing.

And then Christopher spoke, softly, hesitantly at first, and then in a rush. "For a moment...I could feel warmth. I could feel blood rushing through my veins and air in my lungs and muscles and flesh and...you, Maggie. I could feel *you*."

As though his words had released some trigger within her, Maggie found her voice. "It was as though I was on another plane—richer, deeper.... I was here, but I wasn't here, and I could *feel* you, Christopher, I knew your thoughts—"

"Maggie." A single word, quiet, simple, yet explosive with depths of expression that knew no bounds. His eyes were shining, his form was radiant, he worshiped her with a look, as she did him. "The gift you've given me..."

"And you, me..."

They could say no more. They looked at each other, mesmerized with wonder, with joy, overpowered by what they had known and their own inadequacy of expression. And then, slowly, Christopher's expression changed. His eyes were tinted by bewilderment, even a trace of consternation. He took an uncertain step backward.

"I must go," he said.

"Christopher—"

His form began to shimmer, dissolving like dust particles in the wind. Before her eyes, he disappeared.

Chapter Nine

CHRISTOPHER WAS GONE for three days. During that time Maggie tried diligently to recall all those very valid reasons she had once wanted him out of her life. She also tried to dedicate herself with renewed purpose to those elements of a "normal" life she had once held in such esteem, but it was pointless. Her classroom was empty without Christopher's keen observations and bright-eyed interest, her apartment a bleak welcome at the end of the day. She lost her glasses twice and her briefcase once, and Christopher was not there to find them for her. She had popcorn for dinner, and Christopher was not there to chide her.

She had been inside his *soul*. Could she pretend that had never happened? Could she possibly be expected to just step away from that moment, to go on with her life as though it had never been interrupted? She had been a part of him; he was a part of her, in her cells and her senses and swirling through the corridors of her mind like a vaporous breath, constant and gentle and sweet. She was no longer Maggie Castle, plain and ordinary, ruled by logic and comfortable with the routine. She had been a part of another human being, and he had been a part of her, and nothing would ever be ordinary again. She missed Christopher, and she wanted him back desperately.

Sometimes she thought she could feel him nearby; nothing specific, just a tingling at the back of her neck, a slight change in the atmosphere that was no more concrete than the memory of him. Always she would stop, look around and whisper his name. There was never any reply.

There were too many hours to fill and not enough to do within them. She dedicated an entire evening and a good part of a night working on her thesis, and by academic standards she made great headway. But, reading it over, she found herself asking for the first time why she was doing this. What was the point? When she was awarded her doctorate, what would she have gained? Did she really want to spend the rest of her days cloistered among facts and figures in a dull, dry world of intellect and academics? After what she had glimpsed so briefly with Christopher, would she ever be satisfied again with those routines? All her life work had been her center, and achievement her only goal. Now she wondered if any of it was as important as she once had thought.

This new insight into herself shook Maggie profoundly, and the worst was that she could not talk about it with anyone. Christopher would have understood. But Christopher was not there.

She couldn't understand how he could just disappear like that, with no rhyme or reason, no warning or purpose. He had burst into her life, turned it upside down, challenged everything she had ever believed in and threatened the very core of her own self-knowledge...then left. It wasn't fair.

Life went on. She had lessons to prepare, classes to teach, students to tutor, but she bent herself to the tasks with only half her attention. The other half was spent thinking about Christopher, wondering about Christopher, waiting for Christopher. Larry called to ask her for dinner on Saturday night. For the first time since Christopher had come into her life, she couldn't think of an excuse to refuse, so she accepted the invitation.

By Saturday afternoon she was fed up with her own lethargy and self-pity. She decided to take her measuring tape, floor-plan pattern and her collection of paint chips and wallpaper samples over to the new house and spend the afternoon energetically employed. She told herself that immersing herself in the plans for the house was exactly what she needed to take her mind off Christopher. Deep down inside she knew the main reason she wanted to be there was because it was *his* house and being in it would make her feel closer to him.

Although the house was not yet officially hers, Maggie had the key, and with the owners living out of town there was no problem with her going over whenever she wanted. Since meeting Christopher she had had no time—and truthfully, no desire—to engage in outside activities, and, in fact, she had given surprisingly little thought to the house that had begun this entire episode in her life. It was high time, she decided, that she focused on something concrete, something rewarding, something *she* could control.

Autumn moved quickly into winter on the Chesapeake Bay, with bone-chilling damp nights and windy gray days. The air had a heavy taste of oceanside to it as Maggie left her car at the curb and hurried up the drive, and the wind that brushed her cheeks and crept inside her collar felt damp and faintly salty. Dried leaves scuttled across her path, and she pulled her beret down over her ears, shivering in her wool jacket. And yet the house called out to her with welcome and warmth. She could envision a fire crackling and dancing in the grate, yellow lamplight glowing off richly paneled walls, a hint

of cinnamon and spice wafting from the kitchen...
Home. It still felt like home to her.

She unlocked the door quickly and stepped inside.
There was no warming fire on the grate, the shadows in
the foyer were deep, and the entire house held the chill
stillness of disuse. But Maggie did not find the lack of
heat or light foreboding; the house was too filled with
possibilities to allow her to dwell on its current deficits.

She did wish, however, that she had had Larry make
some arrangements to turn on the electricity and the
gas. She wondered whether or not the open fireplaces
worked, and if so, where she could find some fire-
wood. But obviously those amenities would have to wait
for her next visit. Today it was enough to just be here.

She left her canvas bag in the foyer and once again
explored the house. Maggie had half expected the en-
chantment of the place to have worn off by now. Perhaps the house had never been as perfect as she had
imagined; perhaps her inexplicable attraction to it had
been due solely to some sort of magical spell enacted by
the invisible Christopher Durand. But not so. As she
wandered through the house on that bleak October afternoon, she was just as thrilled by it, if not more so,
than she had been on her first tour.

Today, alone, she had the opportunity to notice a
myriad of things that had passed her by the first time.
The artful arrangement of windows in every room, for
example. Not one of them was the same size or style,
but each was designed to admit the maximum light, and
somehow they managed to present a cumulative illusion of unity. The way each room flowed into the next
also impressed her, giving an impression of airiness with
a minimal use of space. Little alcoves were tucked away
here and there, some so cleverly concealed that she ex-

claimed in delight when she discovered them. Brilliant use of optical illusion was everywhere, yet it was so cleverly applied that even Maggie's mathematical mind had difficulty recognizing it at first. Corners were rounded ever so slightly, softening harsh angles and entryways. Some of the walls were actually curved, at such a gentle, almost infinitesimal angle that it was unnoticeable to the casual eye, but the effect was to open up the room to a subtle atmosphere of warmth. What her subconscious had perceived on her first viewing of the house became clear in detail now: This *was* a special place, designed with care and exquisite craftsmanship to present an aura of welcome to all who came here. No wonder she had loved it. If she could have commissioned a modern-day architect to build her dream home, this would have been it.

She ended up in the parlor, gazing out the bay window and smiling to herself with contentment as plans for the house began to form in her mind. She would restore the oversize bathroom to its original condition, she decided, with a big claw-footed tub—perhaps bright red—and even a wooden chain-pull toilet and pedestal lavatory. There would still be room left over for a dressing area with a skirted vanity and a big armoire to hold sheets and towels. Maggie had never before realized a particular fondness for antiques, but now she eagerly looked forward to combing the countryside for rare finds. What a perfect hobby a house like this would be. She would spend the winter cleaning out the garden, and by spring...

"That was the window I always put my Christmas tree in," said a voice behind her.

Maggie's heart stuttered and leaped. She whirled around to find Christopher standing there, and she gasped, both with joy in seeing him and shock for the way he looked. He was dressed in the formal garb of his century—black cutaway, starched white collar and cravat, white gloves and a top hat. He lounged against the doorframe, his expression pleasantly reminiscent, his tone musing as he surveyed the room.

"I did so love the holidays," he went on. "My manservant and I would go out into the woods, cart in wagonloads of greenery and deck this place out to the nines. Garlands and holly boughs and—" his eyes twinkled "—mistletoe, of course, everywhere one looked. A big fir tree would go right where you're standing, and the kitchen women would trim it with gingerbread men and bits of tinsel and paper birds. Do you see that spruce in the center of the yard? I'd hang millet balls and popcorn ropes from it every winter for the birds, and what a feast they would have! I sometimes spent hours watching them. And the parties...ah, this was a gay place during the holidays."

He came forward, gesturing with his arm. "You see how all the doors slide back and each room flows into the other? This entire floor could be made into a ballroom, and I've often accommodated over a hundred guests. I would put the orchestra in the alcove that adjoins the dining room, and the sound carried without a flaw throughout the house. I can still hear the strains of a Strauss waltz if I am quiet enough."

He stopped before her, smiling, and swept off his hat in a deep bow. "Madame, would you care to dance?"

Maggie was glowing with relief and happiness. She couldn't take her eyes off him. "Sir," she said breathlessly, "I would love to."

She took a step toward him, but their hands never touched. Christopher straightened with a shrug and said, "Such foolishness. We can't dance without music."

He tossed his hat into the shadows, but Maggie did not hear it land. *Illusion,* she reminded herself with an effort. *All illusion.*

Christopher turned to her with a sudden twinkle in his eye. "Come with me, Maggie. I want to show you a secret."

He started toward the door, and she had no choice but to follow. "Christopher—what happened? Where have you been?"

"I thought you wanted me to go away," he replied over his shoulder.

Maggie faltered, stumbling a little over her steps just as she did the words. "No. I—I missed you."

Christopher turned, his smile tender and soft and his eyes deep with understanding. "I am always with you," he told her gently. "Even when you can't see me, I'm connected to you. You know that, don't you?"

A slow and certain peace filled Maggie, so simple and so complete that her throat ached with the poignancy of it. She swallowed and after a moment smiled. "Yes," she whispered. "I know."

The answering spark in his eyes was warm and reassuring, then he turned again to lead the way toward the foyer. He stood at the side of the enclosed stairwell and waited for her to catch up. "Now watch," he advised, smiling like a twelve-year-old boy bursting to tell a secret. He lifted his hand and pressed against one corner of the paneling beneath the stairs.

Maggie clapped her hands together in delight as the panel slid back into the wall with a slight creaking sound, revealing an entire, previously hidden room beneath the stairs. "I should have known you'd have designed something like this! Always full of mischief. Wait—I have a flashlight.''

''No need,'' Christopher replied, gesturing her to cross the threshold. ''Come look.''

Only a few cobwebs hung inside the door; Maggie brushed them away with her hand as she stepped cautiously into the secret room. ''My goodness,'' she said softly, looking around.

The room was only a little smaller than the bedroom in her apartment, completely circular, with a sloping ceiling that apparently followed the course of the stairs, but that was never less than eight feet high in any one place. What amazed Maggie was that the room was completely bathed in soft, natural light that sprayed through tiny motes of dust and feathery cobwebs from some source high above her. Maggie bent her head back and turned around in a circle, searching for the source to no avail.

''How did you do that?'' she demanded. ''Where's the light coming from?''

''It's a telescope effect from the skylight upstairs,'' replied Christopher smugly. ''Clever, isn't it?''

Maggie laughed with pleasure. ''I'll say.''

''There isn't a single room in my house that doesn't have some form of natural lighting. Of course, it's much more pleasant in here on a clear day.''

''Oh, I don't know. I like it like it is. Kind of soft and . . . secretive. It's warmer, too.''

''Of course. It's double insulated.''

''Doesn't it get hot in the summer?''

Christopher walked to the left-hand wall and indicated a small wooden pulley. ''This activates an extra set of vents that will admit a marvelous cooling breeze. Of course, if it's a blustery day, they can also turn the place into a wind tunnel.''

"My goodness," Maggie said again, awed. "You were a magician."

"Not at all," he replied modestly. "Just good at what I do."

"And look—your furniture!"

The room was furnished with a comfortable-looking settee in wine brocade, a big, overstuffed reading chair with a hassock and a rolltop desk. A couple of small tables held lamps, and an intricately patterned rug covered the floor. Everything was covered with a thin layer of dust.

"No one has been in here in all these years," Christopher said. "I used to make a game of wondering who would first discover it, but no one ever did."

A magazine lay open on the hassock as though its reader, interrupted in the midst of an article, had set it aside and might be expected to return at any moment. Maggie crossed the room and hesitantly picked it up. The magazine's pages were curled and yellow around the edges; the cover identified it as the December 1899 issue of *The Saturday Evening Post*. Standing there in that secret place, holding something that Christopher had last held over ninety years ago, Maggie felt her throat constrict. Once a living, breathing man had perused these pages, smiling at subtle satire, glancing over advertisements for tonics and buggy wheels and high-button shoes while the faint tinkle of sleigh bells played background music from the lane outside.... He had laid this magazine aside to attend to some other business— a dinner party? A caller at the door?—intending to pick it up again later, but he had never returned. A chill went through Maggie as she stood there, and a wave of overwhelming sorrow. Had he walked from this room to his death? Was she holding in her hands the last item he had touched?

"You're sad," Christopher said suddenly. "I never intended to distress you by bringing you here. I thought it would make you happy."

Maggie looked up at him. The words were difficult to say, but she had to know, now more than ever. "Christopher—how did you die?"

He lifted a quizzical eyebrow. "Didn't I tell you? I'm sure I did." He gave a half shrug. "I was meeting a friend at the station when I spied an infant girl crawling along the tracks just ahead of an oncoming train. Naturally I rushed to intervene and managed to fling the child to safety. But, alas, I was not so fortunate in saving myself. It was over in an instant. The whole town turned out to acclaim me a hero, the mayor awarded me a posthumous medal of honor, and I believe there was even some discussion of erecting a statue in my honor. It was all quite spectacular."

Maggie hesitated, frowning a little while she tried to pinpoint what it was about the story that did not quite ring true. Then she had it. "There aren't any train tracks around here," she pointed out.

"Details," he said dismissively, and at the last minute she caught the mischievous glint in his eyes.

Maggie fought with a grin and lost. It was impossible to feel sorry for him, impossible to hold on to melancholy in his presence. He was not gone. He had not walked out of this room never to return; he had not lost anything. He was as alive and vital this moment as he had ever been, and Maggie was very, very glad.

She put the magazine down and walked over to the desk. She paused with her hands on the roll top. "Do you mind?"

"Please." He made an inviting gesture with his hand. "It's all yours, now."

Feeling a little like a heroine in a children's adventure book sitting down to open a treasure chest, Maggie pushed back the cover on the desk. She pulled out the swivel chair and sat down to examine the contents, exclaiming in delight over the various items she found. There was an ivory-inlaid fountain pen and a porcelain jar filled with dried ink. A neat stack of receipts and handwritten bank drafts—a pair of handmade, Corinthian-leather boots in 1899 cost eight dollars, she noted—and a collection of invitations to dinners, balls and soirees for the holiday season, some from as far away as New York City. She wondered whether the sight of those items brought back memories or regrets for Christopher, but a glance at his face revealed only the mildest interest as he observed her discoveries.

In a bottom drawer she found a sheaf of folded papers that, upon further inspection, proved to be diagrams and notes of some sort. She studied the pages curiously. "What's this?"

Resting one hand on the desk and the other on the back of her chair, Christopher leaned close. "Ah," he said, "now that was a fascinating project. It began through a study I made of the way bats negotiate by using sound rather than sight. It occurred to me that a ship lost in a fog bank might make better use of fog horns if the dispersement of sound waves could be tracked electronically. I was working on a method by which the reflection of sound waves could be directed to move a quill and literally draw a picture of the surrounding coastline. It would have been a big boon to navigation, I think.''

Maggie looked at him in astonishment. ''Radar. You invented radar twenty years before we even had radio.''

He lifted an eyebrow. ''Did I?''

She nodded dully, staring at the diagrams. ''We've been using it since World War II. In ships, airplanes, even automobiles.''

He considered that for a moment, then gave an elaborate, dismissing shrug. ''And there you have it. The world goes gaily on without me, proving that no one man is indispensable.''

A startled laugh escaped her, and she sank back in her chair, regarding him with frank admiration. ''You *are* an extraordinary man.''

It occurred to her to wonder whether his indisputable genius, his simple refusal to accept limitations of any kind, was connected in some way to his presence here now. Surely it would take someone of superlative physical and mental power to survive the decades untarnished as Christopher had done. Perhaps there was a reason, after all, that messages from the Great Beyond most often came from Beethoven or Einstein or Dr. Freud.

She said suddenly, ''Christopher, if you had been born in the twentieth century—that is, if you were actually alive today—what would you be?''

''Do you mean, by profession?'' He hardly spent a moment thinking about it. ''An engineer, I'm certain. Perhaps on your space program.''

She glanced up at him and laughed in simple pleasure. He was no longer dressed in the formal attire of the nineteenth century, but had somehow changed while she wasn't watching into a pair of hip-molding jeans and an open-throated, full-cut, black silk shirt. The effect was wickedly sexy, and for that moment it was easy to imagine him as real and active in the world in which she lived, stepping out of his ghostly shell and assuming a role that was tailor-made for him.

"Perfect," she agreed. "I'd produce the fuel for our next spaceship and you'd design the engine."

"What a team we would make." His eyes picked up a spark of reciprocal delight. "Whoever would have thought that I would have met my match in a woman, and—" a shadow tinted the smile in his eyes with wistfulness as he added softly "—only a century too late."

His regret flowed through her and became her own. Though she dared not give a name to the longing she felt, the sadness or the loss, she felt it as intensely as he did. They held each other's eyes in quiet helplessness for a long moment, and then Maggie had to ask, "Christopher, what happened?" Her voice was tight with pain and uncertainty. "Why did you go away?"

He dropped his gaze briefly to his hand, which rested on the desk—a hand that was slim and strong and shadowed with dark hair at the wrist, a hand so real she could almost feel its warmth, so close she could cover it with her own by moving her fingers only a fraction of an inch. But when she started to do so, Christopher straightened abruptly and stepped away.

"Maggie, my love," he said lightly, "there are some imponderables that are perhaps best left alone."

Tension closed around Maggie's stomach and she searched his face intently. "Tell me," she demanded.

She saw his inner debate, but he could no more lie to her than she could to him. He glanced away and then back again. He said after a moment, reluctantly, "It was not my choice, you should know that. There was a period of time when...I hadn't the energy to make myself visible to you."

Maggie's heart beat with tight, anvillike strokes of dread. "Because I touched you?"

His dark eyes were tender and sober. "Because of what we shared," he corrected. "It was not a natural thing, and one always pays the penalty for breaking the rules."

Maggie nodded slowly, understanding against her will. Christopher was not a physical being, but she had for that moment made him so—just as he, in blending with her, had allowed her the briefest taste of his plane. He could not be in two places at once. He could not be what she was, and she could not be what he was no matter how much they wished differently.

Disappointment closed about her heart, bleak and lonely. It might have been better never to have known that moment with him than to realize now that it could never happen again. But almost immediately Maggie dismissed the self-pitying thought and lifted her chin. He was here, just as he had always been, and there was nothing to regret in that.

"Well," she said, holding his gaze levelly, "now we know. I just won't try to touch you again."

"Perhaps it's for the best," he agreed, but his eyes said differently, and Maggie knew what he was feeling.

She turned to lower the top on the desk. "Thank you for showing me this room, Christopher," she said. "I think it's going to be my favorite place in the house."

"It was mine." Immediately he followed her change of mood. "It occurred to me when I designed it that a man needs a place to escape from his family from time to time, no matter how dearly he loves them. The patter of little feet can get tiresome after a while, even to the most devoted parent.''

Maggie looked up at him in surprise. "But I thought you weren't married.''

"I wasn't. I always expected to be, though.'' And the smallest of puzzled frowns touched his forehead. "Even as I was designing this house, it was as though I were doing it for someone, imagining her likes and dislikes, planning her conveniences, catering to her tastes...and yet she never came along. Silly, wasn't it?''

Then he smiled. "At any rate, it's your house now, and when you start your family, you will always have a place to escape from them.''

Something compelled Maggie to linger on what he had said about the family he had never had, the love he had never found. A measure of poignancy, tenderness and even sorrow was mixed with the relief she felt that he had, in fact, lived here alone. This was her house, and she would not like to think that another woman had once called it her own.

Which was, of course, a ridiculous train of thought, because many women had lived here before Maggie. With an impatient shake of her head she pushed away from the desk and stood up. "I don't intend to marry,'' she told Christopher. "But I'll still enjoy the room.''

"You've said that before,'' Christopher replied dismissively. "That's just female foolishness. Of course you'll marry and have a brood of children to fill up your house. It's the way of nature.''

"Not my nature.'' She took one final look around the room before pulling her gloves out of her jacket pocket and tugging them on. "Will you come out in the garden with me? I want you to tell me exactly what it's supposed to look like.''

"It's only because you haven't found the right man yet." Christopher followed her out of the room, and she watched carefully as he pressed the panel that allowed the door to slide shut again, marveling over the seamless fit. "At your age, I can understand your despair. But you're still healthy and attractive—"

Her burst of laughter cut him short. "Thank you, kind sir! Honestly, you have the most antiquated ideas—which are only natural under the circumstances, I suppose. But I've told you before, people don't have to get married any more, and I choose not to. It's as simple as that."

"Nothing is that simple. Explain it to me."

She spared him a glance of amused exasperation as she pulled open the front door. "I like being alone, that's all."

"No one likes being alone. If you're not coming back in, you'd better take this." He bent to pick up her bag.

"Thank you."

"And lock the door," he reminded her.

"Right." She began the routine search through her purse.

"In your coat pocket?" suggested Christopher.

Maggie thrust her hands into her pockets and came up with the old-fashioned skeleton key. With one dry look at Christopher, she pulled the door closed behind them and turned the lock.

"A case in point," Christopher pointed out mildly. "Two heads are better than one."

"You have a one-track mind, don't you?"

"I'm merely curious."

Across the street, a man in a pea jacket had come out to retrieve his newspaper. He paused, looking at Maggie, and Maggie lifted her hand to him, wondering if he had observed her talking to herself—or worse, heard her. After a moment, the man returned the gesture and went back inside.

Maggie turned up her collar, both as protection against the cold and to hide her face as she started down the steps. The sky was leaden and the wind rattled the dried leaves that clung to overhead branches with an empty, ominous sound. It felt like it was going to snow. Christopher, in his silk shirt and jeans, showed no sign of cold, as, of course, he wouldn't, and that only added to Maggie's uneasiness.

When she was around the side of the building and, hopefully, out of sight of curious eyes, she said, "I don't know why you keep pushing me to get married, anyway. I thought you said you didn't want strangers in your house."

"I am not pushing you. I simply asked a question."

Maggie shivered in the wind and hunched her shoulders, but the frown between her eyes was not purely from physical discomfort. "You don't understand. Things are so complicated today."

"Between men and women," Christopher replied mildly, "things have always been complicated."

They had reached the back garden and he stopped, gazing around with interest. "The roses will have to be trimmed back, of course. There was a flagstone walk that wound through them, I believe, but it's little more than a jungle now. Actually, I had a gardener do all this; I don't remember much about it."

Maggie pulled her scarf tighter around her neck and returned her hands to her pockets, looking over the ragged winter-bare garden without really seeing much of it. "I don't know. Maybe it's because of the way my parents broke up, or maybe it's just in my genes, but

I've always known that permanent relationships were not for me. I don't have what it takes to sacrifice myself for another person, and that's what commitment is all about, isn't it?''

Christopher lifted his arm, gesturing toward the left. "There was a cherry tree there, and some sort of flower bed—tulips in the spring, I think, and something colorful in the summer.''

"I mean, I like being in charge of my own life," Maggie said decisively. "And the only satisfaction I need comes from my work. I learned a long time ago that there are only two things in life I could count on—myself and my work. And that's what I need. Things I can count on. Things that won't collapse under pressure or disappear if you look too closely or disappoint if you expect too much. That's why I became a scientist, don't you see?''

"To escape from the real world?" suggested Christopher.

"Don't be ridiculous. Science is real and solid and permanent. Everything else is unnecessary, a distraction, and I've got enough distractions in my life without a man to complicate it.''

"Love, laughter, pain, disappointment," mused Christopher, "all very distracting, all very complicated—and what a sorry place this world would be without them.''

Before Maggie could reply, he nodded toward the edge of the yard, where a windbreak of spruce trees formed the back border. "There was a willow tree back there, and next to it a gazebo.''

Maggie wanted to pick up the thread of their previous conversation, but something made her hesitate. After a moment she smiled dryly. "A gazebo," she repeated. "I should have known. You're such a romantic."

He looked at her, a peculiar little glint in his eye. "And so are you, Maggie Castle, as you very well know. You may hide behind your textbooks and your formulas, but it's the mystery of the process that seduces you, not the precision. Your closest friend worships rocks, and your mathematics class is liberally laced with references to the lost continent of Atlantis. You collect dragons and unicorns and converse with a spirit and dare to tell me you have no use for anything that isn't practical."

She scowled, uncomfortable with his assessment and with the dim suspicion that he might have stumbled onto a glimmer of truth. "That's not fair. You're the spirit here, and the only reason I converse with you is because you talked to me first."

He smiled and then sobered. "Maggie, love," he said earnestly, "don't ever deny that part of yourself that treasures the impractical, that yearns for the unexplored. Dragons and wizards, castles in the air and all-too-impractical love—those are the things that magic is made of. And believing in magic is the only thing that separates the living from the dying. Rely upon it. This I know."

Maggie looked at him for a moment uncertainly, then turned into the wind and started for her car. But his words stayed with her, nagging at her. Once again, he had given her a great deal to think about. And once again, she did not want to think about it at all.

Chapter Ten

"I HAVE TO STOP by the store and buy stockings," Maggie told him in the car. She had almost said *panty hose*, but decided that the term would be entirely too difficult to explain to a man from the nineteenth century. "I have a dinner date tonight."

"No one I know, I hope."

She glanced at him askance. "Larry."

He masked a pained expression with a sigh. "Ah, well. I suppose even he has to eat."

"You're very inconsistent, you know. First you pester me about getting married, then you object to the men I go out with."

"Not men," Christopher corrected, "man. And the only reason I object to him is that he's not, as one says these days, your type."

"What do you know about my type?"

"He's boring. He's got deeds and mortgages for a heart, and tickertape in place of a soul. He doesn't have the imagination of a fish. He hasn't a fraction of your intellect, but he insists on trying to patronize you. If a woman's self-worth is measured by the company she keeps, you vastly underestimate yourself, and I object to that."

Maggie bristled, but she wasn't sure whether her reaction was in defense of Larry or in defense of herself. "That's the most narrow-minded assessment I've ever heard. You don't even know him. Larry has a lot of fine qualities, and furthermore, opposites sometimes attract, you know."

"He doesn't have enough character to be your opposite," Christopher retorted. "And if he is the best example you can find of a twentieth-century man, I would say it's a fine thing you've decided not to marry. Why propagate the species?"

"Oh, for heaven's sake!"

"Besides," Christopher added mildly, "you don't love him, and you never will. The entire relationship is a gargantuan waste of time."

Maggie wished she had a snappy rejoinder for that, but the truth was she was already beginning to regret having made the date with Larry. Now that Christopher was back she far preferred to spend the evening with him, and every minute she spent doing anything else did seem like a waste of time. As a matter of fact, if Christopher hadn't goaded her about Larry, she probably would have found a way to call off the date. But now pride—and perhaps a touch of sheer contrariness—was forcing her to keep it.

There was a shopping mall on the way home, and as she pulled into the parking lot, Christopher's quick enthusiasm over the sights and sounds immediately took the edge off her irritation. Before long she abandoned herself to a childlike sense of adventure as they toured the facility together, spraying perfume samples into the air for his pleasure, stifling laughter at the comments he made about the other shoppers, enjoying his absorbed study of comparative technology in the small-appliances department. No wonder he called Larry boring. Anyone would be boring in comparison to Christopher.

As Maggie was preparing to leave, panty hose in hand, Christopher suddenly stopped and indicated a mannequin clad in a striking violet outfit. The skirt was short and full, the hip-length jacket cinched with a wide red belt. A red scarf was tossed jauntily over the shoulder.

"That violet is the exact color of your eyes," Christopher said.

"It's pretty," Maggie agreed, murmuring so as not to be overheard.

But a salesclerk, approaching from her right, heard anyway. "Yes it is, isn't it?" she said brightly. "Would you like to try it on?"

Maggie was embarrassed. "Oh, I don't think so—"

"Try it on," urged Christopher.

"I'm sure we have your size."

"It's really not my style—"

"What do you know about style?" scoffed Christopher. "You're a scientist."

The salesclerk, flipping through the rack, came up with Maggie's size. "This should do, I think."

"I haven't worn a skirt that short since I was three years old," Maggie said dubiously.

"And that's one thing I've never understood," Christopher commented. "You have a fine figure—which," he assured her with a twinkle, "I am in a position to know. So why do you persist in hiding it behind all those unattractive layers of clothing?"

Maggie started to scowl at him, caught the salesclerk's puzzled look and then had no choice but to accept the outfit. "I guess it wouldn't hurt to try it on."

"The dressing room is this way."

Christopher started to follow, but stopped, grinning, at the look Maggie cast him over her shoulder. "I'll wait outside," he offered.

Maggie changed quickly, feeling a little foolish for allowing herself to be roped into this. She didn't want a new outfit and couldn't imagine herself ever wearing anything like this. The price tag was more than a little intimidating, and she was just wasting time. She should have known better than to let herself get caught up in Christopher's enthusiasm.

But when Maggie tightened the belt, straightened the skirt and turned to the full-length mirror, she caught her breath at what she saw. "My goodness," she said softly.

"Brava!" said Christopher behind her.

There was no reflection in the mirror, but when she whirled, Christopher was sitting on the small stool behind her, his hand linked around one knee, his eyes alight with approval. "Maggie, my dear, you look stunning."

She turned hesitantly back to the mirror and saw only the empty stool reflected there. After all this time, she thought she had gotten used to Christopher's tricks, but a chill of uneasiness ran down her spine. Then and there she decided she would have no mirrors in her new house.

She had to agree with him about the outfit, though. She looked like a different person—younger, vibrant, carefree. Her eyes sparkled, and even her hair seemed shinier, streaked with clear, golden highlights. The big belt made her waist look nonexistent, and her legs, which had always been slender, were flattered by the playful cut of the skirt. Maggie, who had always had better things to think about than clothes and who, in fact, had never cared much one way or the other what she looked like, suddenly began to see herself in a whole new light.

"Elena," she decided, "would definitely approve."

"What do you think?" called the clerk from outside the door.

"Ask her to bring in the yellow one," Christopher suggested.

"It's perfect," Maggie called back. "I love it."

"The yellow one," Christopher insisted.

Maggie gave him a frustrated look, but she could hardly argue with him while the clerk was standing only inches away, so she made the request.

Over the next half hour Maggie tried on six new outfits, each one more flattering than the last. The clerk, sensing a major sale, brought in an array of accessories and shoes that transformed a collection of dresses and slacks into a whole new wardrobe. Maggie felt like Cinderella, and she could not remember ever having had so much fun.

"But," she whispered to Christopher when the clerk had disappeared to find the perfect pin for a challis shirtwaist, "I can't buy all this. For one thing, I can't afford it—"

"Use your plastic credit," replied Christopher, unconcerned.

She made a face. "Even plastic has to be paid for sometime."

Christopher held up an aqua silk blouse, admiring the way the dressing room spotlights filtered through the gauzy material. "On my desk," he said absently, "anchoring a stack of unanswered letters, is a pewter cup. If you had bothered to examine it, you would have recognized it as a Paul Revere. It was quite valuable in 1890. I'm sure it must have appreciated some by now. It surely should be enough to pay for all this."

Maggie stared at him. "Are you kidding? What other surprises do you have in store?"

He favored her with an enigmatic smile. "Enough, I hope, to keep you pleasantly entertained for some time to come."

Maggie was torn between the sheer hedonistic pleasure of the colorful wools, silks and gauzes piled around her and her ultimate practical nature, and for a moment, the debate was close. At last she shook her head and began to return the garments to their hangers.

"That's not the point. I have no use for any of this. I'm not a clotheshorse. It was fun pretending but—"

"Is having fun a crime?"

"Of course not, it's just that—"

"You're being practical again. A fine thing in moderation, but you're running the risk of becoming as dull as dear old Larry." The charm of Christopher's smile diffused any retort she might have liked to make to his last comment. "Relax, be frivolous. Enjoy yourself. You're worth every penny you'll spend on these lovely things and more."

The temptation was great, and his argument convincing, but Maggie stubbornly held on to her last shred of resistance. "I don't know why you're so interested anyway," she muttered, caressing the fold of a butter-soft suede skirt with unconscious sensuous delight. "I'm the one who has to wear these things."

"Because," replied Christopher cheerfully, "as I've told you many times before, I have a weakness for beautiful things. And while you've always been beautiful to me, your pleasure in your own appearance makes you glow even brighter. And that makes me very, very happy."

Maggie hid her smile from him, but her decision was made. Beautiful was not a term she often heard applied to herself, and no one had ever been able to make her believe it before. But then, Christopher made her believe a great many things she had never thought possible before: ghosts and dragons and subtle magic; that she was beautiful; that he was real.... So much inside of Maggie had changed since Christopher had come into her life, it only made sense that the outside should change, as well.

She glanced at Christopher, half coy, half skeptical, "Beautiful, hmm?"

"Absolutely. So beautiful, in fact, that if you had not already made up your mind to remain single, I believe I'd marry you."

Maggie laughed out loud with delight, then quickly smothered the sound lest the curious salesclerk return. "A lot of good that would do you—or me, either, as a matter of fact." And then, giving in to a rare flirtatious impulse, she added, "What would you do if you could marry me?"

His eyes danced, and he spread his hands expansively. "Why, dear heart, I would give you the world wrapped in a silver ribbon. I would toast you with champagne on the Champs Elysées. I would declare my passion for you from atop the pyramids of Giza. I would discover a star and name it for you."

She smothered another giggle, and the playfulness in his eyes deepened into a tender smile as he added, "I would be the cleverest, most entertaining husband who ever lived, because living would be pointless if I could not hear you laugh like that at least once an hour."

A little self-consciously, Maggie brought her fingers to her lips, where a smile still lingered, and his eyes followed the gesture. A warming color touched her cheeks that had to do with little more than the gentle, absorbing light in Christopher's eyes. And as he looked at her, that light focused into something richer, something deeper, something that caused her to catch her breath as he added softly, "I would fill your world with magic dragons and fanciful castles, and I would cherish you, with all my heart and soul, for all eternity."

Maggie's heart was throbbing in her throat. Her chest ached with suspended breath and with a yearning, deep, intense and painful, that she dared not name. Slowly, Christopher lifted his hand as though to touch her face, and Maggie's fingers moved, straining toward him.

And then Christopher dropped his hand. He said huskily, "I beg you not to settle for less from any man, Maggie, love."

The salesclerk tapped on the door. Maggie turned, and when she glanced in the mirror, Christopher was not there. But her face was flushed, and her heart was pounding, and the ache inside her did not go away.

MAGGIE MANAGED TO CONVINCE herself that she really did want to go out with Larry that night. Somehow it seemed safer than staying home alone with Christopher, though when she tried to analyze what *safe* meant, she came away puzzled and embarrassed by her own foolishness.

She took special care with her appearance, choosing from her new wardrobe a form-fitted cream-colored dress with a scooped neckline and a flared skirt—not because she particularly wanted to impress Larry, but because she found, to her surprise, that she actually enjoyed dressing up. She pinned up her curls in back, fluffing her hair around her face for a fuller, more elegant look, and even experimented with a new peach lipstick and taupe eyeshadow. She accessorized the outfit with long gold chains and bangle bracelets and stood before the mirror, smoothing the dress over her curves and admiring the effect as she turned this way and that.

"I look terrific," she decided.

"You look spectacular," Christopher corrected.

When Maggie turned, his eyes were glinting with the frank appreciation of an unbiased male, and a tingling glow started at the tip of Maggie's stylishly-clad toes and spread to her cheeks. She swept him a curtsy. "You are too generous."

"And you're more than that stuffed shirt deserves."

"Don't start that again." She glanced at her watch and began a hurried search for her purse. Then she stopped and looked at Christopher with concern. "Listen—you're not going to hang around and make trouble tonight, are you? Because if you are—"

He lifted his hand. "I'll be the picture of a well-deported gentleman."

She found her purse behind the cushion of a club chair. "I'd rather you be the picture of an invisible gentleman."

"And leave you to the mercy of that bag of wind? You'll expire of boredom before the evening's half done."

"Christopher..."

"Oh, very well. I'll leave you alone. But remember, you asked for it."

The doorbell rang, and Maggie hurried to answer it, casting Christopher a warning glance as she went. "Remember..."

Christopher shrugged acquiescence and turned away as she pulled open the door.

Larry's eyes lit with surprise as he looked at her. "You look nice," he said.

"What a gift for words the man has," Christopher muttered.

Maggie ignored him as she brushed Larry's cheek with a kiss. "I look spectacular," she corrected pertly. "I went shopping today."

"So I see." Larry stepped inside. "Elena finally got to you, did she?"

"Not exactly. Just let me get my coat."

"You're not going to offer me a drink?"

"You don't think I got all dressed up just to sit around my apartment, do you? I want to be taken out and shown off!"

Larry brushed the top of her hair with a kiss as he helped her into her coat. "That will be my pleasure."

"Don't worry about me." Christopher dropped to the sofa and picked up the remote control. "I'll find a way to entertain myself. Have a good time."

Maggie cast a harried glance at him, and Larry's head whipped around as the television flared to life. "What—" Larry demanded.

"The cat," Maggie said quickly, grabbing his arm and ushering him to the door. "The cat must have stepped on the remote control."

"What cat? You don't have a cat—"

"A new cat. I just got him. He's a menace, really...." Maggie breathed a sigh of relief as she firmly closed and locked the door behind her.

Larry bought her story about the stray cat she had taken in, and by the time they reached the restaurant, Maggie had begun to relax. She knew, of course, that Christopher wasn't really safe at home, watching television, that in all likelihood he was hovering over her shoulder observing every move and making snide comments to himself. But as long as she couldn't see him, she didn't worry about him, and it was easy to maintain the illusion of privacy.

The restaurant was small and candlelit, the ambience intimate and familiar. It had become a favorite place of Maggie's and Larry's in the time they had been seeing each other, and Maggie was surprised at how good it felt to be back in comfortable surroundings after the unplanned course her life had taken in the last few weeks. She sat back with a glass of wine and let the accumulated tension seep out of her muscles.

Larry smiled at her across the table. "God, it's good to see you—and not just because you look so spectacular." He emphasized the last word slightly. "It seems like ages."

"That's the nice thing about us, isn't it?" Maggie agreed easily. "We can go for weeks without seeing each other or even thinking about each other every day. But when we get together again it's always so comfortable. We just pick up where we left off."

Larry reached across the table and covered her hand with his. "I do think about you every day," he said softly. "I just know better than to crowd you. I miss you, Maggie."

Maggie was touched. He was a nice man. Thoughtful, dependable, loyal.... But she also felt a twinge of guilt because she could not answer in kind. She enjoyed being with Larry, and she did appreciate all his commendable attributes. But she did not miss him the way she missed Christopher when he was gone.

"So." She took a sip of her wine. "How is everything going with the house closing? Any problems?"

"Oh, before I forget." Larry reached for his overcoat on the hook beside the booth and took out a folded manila envelope. "Here's that information on the history of the house you asked for. You know Cecile, the perpetual overachiever. She's got copies of deeds and records and newspaper clippings for the past hundred years in here. There's even some stuff on the original builder of the house. I didn't get a chance to look at it, but Cecile thought you might find it interesting."

"Great." Maggie took the packet and slipped it into her purse. She doubted whether Larry's secretary had been able to find anything about Christopher she didn't already know, but she would make a point of reading through the material when she had a chance. "Be sure to thank her for me."

"As you said, it made her feel useful. I have to go to Los Angeles next week, so if it's all right with you, Jeff will handle your closing." Jeff was one of the agents in Larry's office. "I've done all the ground work, and everything should be purely routine from now on. The papers will arrive by mail, and all you have to do is come into the office and have someone notarize your signature. The inspection turned out fine, by the way. Jeff has everything on file, if you want to look at it."

"No, all I want to do is move in. What do you have to do in Los Angeles?"

While the salad was served, he told her about a seminar combined with a property-buying expedition that might take two or three weeks. Maggie smiled and nodded at the appropriate times, but she really didn't pay much attention. Her mind strayed, and she found herself imagining that the person who sat opposite her had dark hair and soft brown eyes, that his voice was lyrically accented and his conversation liberally sprinkled with acid-sharp wit . . . That his smile was a slow, sensuous curve of the lips, and his hand, when it closed over hers, was strong and slender and warm and sent a thrill of vibrant awareness to every nerve fiber in her body.

The imaginings made her heart beat faster, and an uncomfortable tightness gathered in her stomach. She was ashamed of herself for fantasizing about Christopher while dining with Larry, and embarrassed because it seemed like such an adolescent thing to do. A certain wistfulness lingered that she could not entirely dismiss. *If only,* she thought as the main course was served, *if only it could be Christopher here with me, enjoying the food, being supercilious to the waiter, making me laugh with his stories.... Smiling at me in that way he has, so all the world seems to disappear except for the two of us. Holding my coat for me as we leave, touching me... Touching me.*

A wave of overwhelming poignancy struck her at the unfairness of it all, and she had to put down her fork. The seafood pasta, which only a moment ago had been so appetizing, now looked dull and tasteless. It should be Christopher with her. She wanted it to be Christopher. Christopher, so handsome and urbane, so charming and amusing and full of the lust for life. Christopher, who understood her so well, who challenged and soothed her and made her feel more alive and important and vital than anyone had ever done before. Christopher, with whom every moment was a moment to be remembered, perfect in every way... except one.

Larry asked, "What's wrong?"

She looked up, startled and guilty, and gave him a quick smile. "Nothing. I was just thinking—how nice this is. I'm glad you asked me out." And that was the truth. She had enjoyed Larry's companionship for almost two years and had never regretted a moment of it.

It was Larry she should be thinking about, she reprimanded herself determinedly, not some phantom who could never offer her more than what-might-have-been.

Larry's hand closed over her knee beneath the small table. It was a gentle clasp, warm and intimate, and it meant no more to Maggie than a friendly pat on the head. He said, "And I'm glad you accepted. I wasn't sure you would, you know."

Her guilt was compounded, and she began to apologize. "I know I've been a little offhand lately—"

"No, it's okay. I told you before, I'm a patient man." He smiled. "You know I'd like nothing better in the world than for you to come with me to California."

And before she could think of a protest, he added, "I know you can't get the time off, and in a way it's just as well. I intend to do some thinking while I'm gone, and I hope you will, too."

She couldn't keep the slight note of trepidation out of her tone as she asked, "About what?"

"About us." His expression was serious. "About what we mean to each other, and what our future is."

As she drew a breath, his hand tightened on her knee. "Just think about it, Maggie," he urged. "We're good together, you know that. We think alike, we value the same things. We balance each other in so many ways. Do you know how rare that is?"

Maggie hesitated, then smiled a little. "We hardly ever fight," she agreed.

He relaxed. "And when we do, I let you win."

"An admirable characteristic in a man."

"Dynasties have been built on less."

Maggie chuckled, remembering why she liked Larry. He was easy to be with, as comfortable as an old shoe, and there were worse things, weren't there? Why was she being so hard on him?

"Well, I'm not interested in building a dynasty," she told him, picking up her fork again, "but I am having a good time. Are we ordering dessert?"

"Only if you promise to think about us while I'm gone."

She hesitated, then smiled. "Okay, I promise. It can't do any harm to think, can it?"

"I'm hoping," he returned gently, "that it will do a lot of good."

The old familiar camaraderie settled over them for the remainder of the meal, and Maggie was glad she had come. There were minutes at a time when she did not think about Christopher at all, except to be grateful that he had kept his word and was leaving them alone, and she diligently avoided making further comparisons between the two men. As they lingered over amaretto coffee, it seemed only natural that Larry should take her hand and say, "Come home with me, Maggie. Stay the night. It's going to be a long time before we see each other again. Too long."

Maggie hesitated. The evening had been so pleasant, so unstrained and easy, that it was understandable to want to continue it. Comfortable. That was the way everything was with Larry, and she needed to be comfortable for a while, to relax and forget inexplicable phenomena and demanding puzzles of the heart. It would have been easy to say yes. She almost wanted to say yes.

But Christopher intruded. Christopher, who was always with her, who would always know. Who, even when she couldn't see him, was lodged inside her mind. She had no privacy now. How could she lie in one man's arms while dreaming of the dark soulful eyes of another? How could she pretend it was fair to Larry or herself or even to Christopher? How had her life gotten so complicated, and would it ever be simple again?

She looked at Larry and tried to smile. "I'm sorry, Larry. Tonight isn't good for me."

She left it at that, and Larry, though he was visibly disappointed, perhaps even hurt, accepted it. But Maggie was bitterly disappointed—and for a reason that went much deeper than the fact that she was going home alone.

Chapter Eleven

MAGGIE CLOSED THE DOOR behind her and called softly, "Christopher?"

She touched the switch by the door, and the room sprang to light. Christopher was leaning against the back of the sofa, his legs crossed at the ankles, his palms braced behind him. "You should have invited him up for coffee," he said.

Maggie slipped out of her coat and hung it on the coatrack. "I didn't want to."

"But you had a good time." It was a statement, not a question, and Christopher was watching her with an odd, almost quizzical expression on his face.

"Yes, I did." Maggie tried not to sound defensive as she stepped out of her shoes and left them by the door. "A very good time."

Christopher straightened up, his tone subdued. "I suspect I owe you an apology. You do like the fellow, don't you?"

Maggie looked at him, a little taken aback by the question and half tempted to take advantage of it. But she couldn't.

All day they had been sparring around each other, touching highs and lows and dancing around the real issues. No, it was longer than just one day; for every moment of truth there'd been a moment of laughter, a question left unanswered, a problem ignored, and it had been going on forever. But something had changed. The music had run down, and the time for dancing was over. Their defenses were gone, and only the raw truth remained.

She sighed and ran her fingers through her hair, as though she could clear away the confusion that clung to her as easily as she dislodged pins and curls. "The truth is," she admitted tiredly, "I spent most of the evening thinking about you."

"Excuse me?"

He seemed genuinely surprised, and Maggie allowed herself a small smile. Sometimes she forgot that the ability to read minds was not among his supernatural powers.

"Thinking about how unfair everything is and making comparisons...between you and Larry. Larry didn't come off too well." She flung herself onto the sofa, stretched out and put her feet on the coffee table, leaning her head back wearily. "You know what your problem is, don't you? You're too perfect. No one stands a chance against you. You're so damn perfect, I sometimes think I dreamed you."

He smiled gently. "To me, Maggie love, everything is a dream—except you."

Pain clutched at her chest, and she squeezed her eyes closed against it. "Oh, Christopher, why did it have to be me you decided to haunt? Everything was so simple before. I knew who I was and what I wanted. I made my decisions and I stuck to them. And now... Now I don't know anything anymore."

He was silent for such a long time that Maggie opened her eyes and twisted her head around to look at him. The witty dismissal or arrogant rebuff she had half expected to find forming on his features was noticeably absent; instead, there was the same sort of weary resignation in his eyes that she was feeling.

"It was not to bring you pain," he said quietly. "That much I know." And then he sighed, one corner of his lips curving into a wry smile. "Ah, Maggie. I remember the awakening, when you walked into the house that first day. Aeons of cobwebs clearing from my mind, echoes of life all around me . . . and the joy. I can't tell you of the joy when I first began to understand what was happening to me."

For a moment his eyes lit with remembrance of that joy, and Maggie's heart began to speed in empathetic reaction. His hands opened and then curled with the intensity of his effort to find the right words as he went on. "The beauty of those first days of discovery and rediscovery . . . it was as though the hungry dreams of a thousand lonely souls had been suddenly brought to life. I thought if man could create his own heaven, this must be it. But now—" he closed his eyes, and his lips were traced with a faint, sad smile "—I think what I must have created is hell."

Maggie drew in a breath, but no words came. She pulled her legs beneath her and grasped the back of the sofa, turning fully to look at him, helpless, silently straining toward him.

He opened his eyes, but the sad smile lingered. "You know the story of Tantalus in Hades. To want and not to have is torment. But to be within inches of holding in your hand the very essence of life and to know it will never be yours . . . that is hell. You are life to me, Maggie," he said simply.

The swollen bud of yearning inside her suddenly burst into flower, sweet, expansive, aching with simple beauty and thirsting for recognition. Possibilities and impossibilities merged into one, and the thoughts she had kept so carefully buried inside her suddenly demanded words.

She clutched the back of the sofa tightly; she whispered, "Oh, Christopher! I wish—"

Swiftly, he was beside her, his finger uplifted as though to still her lips. But he did not touch her. "I know what you wish." His voice was gentle, sonorous, and his expression was so tender that looking at it twisted her heart. But in his eyes was a warning. "And you know I wish the same thing. But we both know it's insanity." He managed a small, unconvincing smile. "After all, the two of us give a whole new meaning to the term worlds apart, don't we?"

No, Maggie thought, and her fingers dug fiercely into the back of the sofa. No, it's not fair.... "I want to touch you," she said. Her voice trembled, and she searched his face desperately, aching with what she saw reflected there. "I want to hold you, to be near you.... I want you to be real, Christopher."

"Maggie." A simple word, barely a breath, and the world seemed to hover on the edge of upheaval. His hand lifted, cupping the air near the side of her face, so close that she could feel the static-electric charge that presaged his touch. His gaze seemed to go through her, probing within her, gathering bits of her soul...and leaving her empty.

He dropped his hand. "I wish," he said softly, "that I could give something to you to make up for all the pain I've caused."

And then his face grew shielded, and he dropped his eyes. Slowly he turned away from her, his voice flat. "But, of course, I can't. Perhaps it would be best if, in the morning, we forgot we ever spoke of this."

And just like that, the door closed. The expectancy, the wild hope, the desperate, irrational yearning drained out of Maggie in a slow stream and left her deflated. "Yes," she said dully.

He was right. It was insanity. Futile, hopeless insanity. She felt as though she should be ashamed of her own weakness, but she had not the energy even for that. She stood up. "I'm very tired. I'm going to bed."

Christopher did not answer, but she did not expect him to. A well of emptiness followed her to bed, and she did not look forward to the long night ahead.

She was not aware of falling asleep, but the exhaustion of depression overtook her. Too many complicated, unwelcome concepts wrestled in her mind; she could not possibly deal with them all, and her body's natural defense mechanism took over, seeking escape in sleep. But it was a fretful, unnatural sleep that was more tiring than restful, filled with fitful images and elusive dreams, and even in the deepest slumber she longed for morning.

She was almost relieved when something woke her... or almost woke her. The night had left her drugged with fatigue, and she could not open her eyes, could barely turn her head. Gradually she became aware that what had disturbed her had been a movement, like a weight on her bed. She had vague thoughts of an intruder and searched through the foggy shroud of sleep for a feeling of alarm. But then she remembered Christopher and brought up some dim, disconnected reassurances that Christopher would protect her. With a soft, half-questioning, half-contented sound, she started to sink into sleep again.

She felt a touch on her forehead. Soft, whispery, lovely. She tried to open her eyes but couldn't. She didn't really even want to. The stroking caress cupped her cheek. She murmured, "Christopher?"

"Yes, love. It's me."

She wanted to wake up; she didn't want to wake up. Caught in the netherland between dreams and daylight, questions faded. It was Christopher. She was glad.

And then there was a brush of breath across her lips, the butterfly touch of a kiss. Lovely, so lovely. The touch again of lips upon her throat, slow golden pleasure. She wanted to lift her arms, to embrace and return the caress, but her limbs were like lead weights. She let herself sink into the soft, hazy bliss.

"I'm dreaming, aren't I?"

She wasn't sure whether she said the words or merely thought them. But Christopher's voice was like a melody, rich and soft and mesmeric.

"Don't wake, love. Let me give this night to you...to us."

A dream, but more than that. For it was Christopher, and she felt his touch, she tasted his kiss. The silky brush of his hair against her cheek, the smooth, pliant texture of his skin. His fingers were like poetry on her flesh, delicate, warm, arousing. His touch played over her breasts and stroked the line of her rib cage and her waist, his caress moved aside the material of her nightgown, baring her naked thighs, cupping her hips. Sensuality in its purest, most natural form engulfed her, nuances of sensation she had never imagined before were explored to their finest extension, and she let herself drown in them.

Desire was rich and deeply textured, building toward a pinnacle that glowed like a jewel in the distant fog. But the edges of sensation were blurred, like a film shot in soft focus. There were no sharp stabs of unfulfilled longing, no fevered gasps of passion; there was only pleasure without pain. At times she seemed to lift her arms, embracing the shape of his lean, muscled back, threading the satiny tips of his hair through her fingers, feeling the heat and texture of his naked skin beneath her palms. At other times she was suffused in the pleasure he brought her, her arms and legs distant things with no will of their own, responsive only to the exquisite sensation of his touch.

She tasted the warm hollow of his neck with her tongue; she inhaled the scent of him that could not then, nor ever, be defined. There was a long, delicate moment when all sensation was concentrated upon the meeting of their fingers, stroking, entwining, discovering, memorizing. She felt his warmth engulfing her, his love glowing through her, around her and inside her. She felt the pressure of his thighs, strong and muscled, against hers, and their joining.... More than a joining. It was a blending of physical sensation and higher truth, golden waves of rapture, gentle ecstasy, endless, spinning delight. They were one; they always had been and always would be. So simple, so lovely, so true.

There was never a moment to mark the ending of the dream. A sensation that went beyond pleasure lingered within her like an ethereal glow, sure and solid, not fading or changing even as the heaviness of a deeper sleep crept up to embrace her. She could feel the pillow beneath her head and the slow steady beating of her heart. And she could feel his fingers entwined with hers, his warmth, his presence, next to her. A part of her struggled to awake, wanted to know, begged to let her waking senses confirm what her dreaming mind knew. But a deeper, and perhaps wiser, part of her refused the instinct.

"I can still feel you," she whispered—or thought. "Your pulse beating inside my skin, your breath on my lips...a part of me. Still a part of me."

The whisper of a kiss brushed her hair. "Always," he said softly. "Always."

WHEN MAGGIE AWOKE the next morning the memories of the night were clear, and Christopher was with her. She knew he was near even before she opened her eyes, and when she turned in bed, focusing against the diffuse light that streamed through her sheer curtains, she saw him.

He was perched upon the edge of her dresser, wearing jeans and a white sweatshirt, watching her with a drowsy smile. "You are lovely when you sleep. All those cares and tensions you carry with you during the day disappear by night, and you are as innocent as an angel. I wonder if that's true of everyone."

Maggie sat up slowly, her hand going automatically to the front closure of her nightgown, which had come slightly awry during the night but which left nothing indecently exposed. At first she was embarrassed, then she felt foolish. And then she looked into Christopher's gentle brown eyes and knew she had no cause for either of those emotions.

Nothing had changed. And everything had changed. Deep inside a treasured part of her heart, the glow remained, the memory of touching and being touched. It had begun almost a week ago, when she had pressed her palm against Christopher's and transformed them both; it had expanded last night into a dream that was more than a dream. She had given away a part of herself, she had accepted a part of him in return. No, she wasn't the same. She had touched his soul. How could she ever be the same again?

She said, a little hesitantly. "I dreamed about you last night."

He held her gaze, tenderly and with great care. "I dreamed about you, too."

She released a breath that was shaky and uncertain, yet filled with wonder. "It—was only a dream."

He smiled. "Of course. What else could it be?"

"A dream—that you gave to me."

He was silent.

Doubts and frustration struggled to the surface, nagging at her like pinpricks. "But Christopher—how can that be?"

He hesitated, then said, "Are you sorry to have dreamed of me?"

"No," she said immediately, almost breathing the word. "No." And she realized in a rush that it was true. The whys and hows no longer mattered—if they ever had. All that mattered was that Christopher was here, a part of her life, just as he should be. Just as, it seemed, he had always been.

She smiled a little shyly. "I'm glad I met you, Christopher."

"And I'm glad I found you," he replied soberly.

And it occurred to Maggie, as she sat there awash in contentment and the light of a new day, that that was the first time they had ever said those words to each other. It seemed long overdue.

THE HOUSE WAS OFFICIALLY Maggie's on the twelfth of November. From that day onward she spent every spare moment with Christopher at the house, stripping, refurbishing, painting and papering. They pored over catalogs together, they debated over colors, they bantered and argued and laughed a great deal; they shared secrets and told stories and passed quiet moments of peaceful companionship. Those were the happiest, most fulfilling weeks of Maggie's life.

Larry called several times from the West Coast, and Maggie took his calls almost absently, saying what was expected without giving the conversation—or Larry—much thought. Elena left messages on her answering machine, which Maggie rarely bothered to return. Other friends and acquaintances called to ask her to lunch or dinner, but Maggie wasn't interested. She stopped working on her thesis; the cold practical world of theories and mathematics had lost its appeal for her. She gave up her private tutoring sessions with the excuse that she really didn't have the time. The truth was that every moment distracting her from Christopher was, to her, a waste of time. And when she looked back, in rare moments of introspection, to the time before Christopher had come into her life, she could not imagine how she had ever considered herself happy, her work challenging, her life satisfying. Everything before Christopher seemed like a shadow of what it now was.

"I am not at all sure," Christopher said, studying the wall sconces on either side of the fireplace in the newly painted parlor, "that I like electricity as much as I once did. Gas light was much more romantic."

"Forget it." Maggie examined a minute chip in the paint the electrician had left when installing the sconces, and then decided with a little touch up it wouldn't show at all. "I agreed to gas heat, but gas light is out of the question."

She stepped back and observed the fireplace area with a critical eye. The warm melon walls made the room glow, the white moldings and shiny hardwood floors added crisp contrast. The wall sconces were a perfect touch. She only wished she could do something about that ugly gas heater.

"Are you sure we can't open up the fireplace in here?"

"Darling, you'd freeze. Even I had coal-burning stoves in most of the rooms. I only left this fireplace open because I rarely used the parlor in winter. You'll just have to put a screen in front of the heating unit if it bothers you."

"No chance of central heat, huh?"

"Absolutely not. There's no telling what kind of structural damage would be done if you tried to install it, and the cost, I assure you, would be prohibitive. The entire building would have to be rewired—"

"Hello! Anybody home?"

"Elena!" Maggie turned in surprise and delight just as the other woman appeared at the door of the parlor.

"I knocked, but you didn't hear me— My goodness, look at you! Look at this place! I don't know which to gush over first!"

Laughing, Maggie crossed the room and gave her friend a hug. "What in the world are you doing here? How did you find me?"

"Well, it seemed to me if the mountain wouldn't come to Mohammed . . ." Elena flung back the folds of her stylish black cape and held Maggie's hands, her eyes dancing as she looked at her friend. "What have you done to yourself? You look marvelous!"

In her bright yellow coveralls, emerald sweater and striped painter's hat, Maggie posed for her friend's inspection. "Like my new look?"

"You could have stepped right off the cover of *Seventeen*."

Maggie made a face. "I'd rather you'd said *Cosmo*."

Elena laughed. "You've got a way to go for that, sweetie. But it's more than the clothes—you're practically glowing." Then she looked at her suspiciously. "You're not pregnant, are you?"

"You always did say the wildest things. Can't a person have a good time without arousing your dirty little mind?"

"You must be," agreed Elena, letting her cape and purse drop to the floor. "Having a good time, that is. You don't answer your phone, no one ever sees you anymore...." She stepped forward, using the same appraising eye on the room that she had on Maggie. "So this is what all the fuss is about. Incredible, absolutely incredible."

"A woman of discriminating taste," observed Christopher. He stepped back, leaning against the fireplace, as Elena wandered around.

"It's beautiful, Maggie," she said, turning. "You can't tell me you've done this all yourself?"

"Well, not exactly. I had professionals in to do the floors and some of the technical work."

"Give her the tour," suggested Christopher.

"It's not anywhere near finished yet," Maggie said. "I've hardly even started upstairs. But if you'd like to see—"

"Do you think I came all the way just to have you tell me about it? I'm dying to see!"

Elena was a perfect first guest. Maggie had forgotten how much she enjoyed the other woman's enthusiastic company, and she began to feel guilty for not returning Elena's phone calls. She had missed her friend, more than she realized until this moment. Elena admired the layout of the rooms and the precision of the craftsmanship much as Maggie first had done; she exclaimed over the bedroom Maggie had started redecorating and mentioned several antique shops she couldn't wait to show her friend.

In the downstairs foyer again, Elena said, "I'm going to give you an amethyst cluster for your housewarming. It will look stunning on a little table right in front of the window there, and it'll also protect your house from burglars and tornados."

Christopher chuckled. "I like your friend. She has style."

Elena looped her arm through Maggie's, walking back toward the parlor. "Well, I can certainly see why you fell in love with this place. You're going to have an absolute showplace when you're finished. And it doesn't look the least bit haunted."

Maggie glanced at her, startled, but Elena went on blithely, "Whoever would have thought you'd turn out to be the domestic type? Painting, wallpapering, plastering...I thought the only kind of pattern you ever got excited about was on graph paper. But I'm so glad for you, Maggie." She squeezed her hand, smiling. "You've always been such a workaholic, I was really worried about you. But this is just what you needed."

"You're right," agreed Maggie, and the relief she felt at having Elena's approval for the new direction her life was taking surprised her. "I've never had as much fun as I have with this house. But it's more than fun—it's real satisfaction, do you know what I mean?"

"Absolutely. There's more to life than sums and quotients."

Maggie nodded agreement. "I've even put off working on my doctorate, did you know that?"

Now it was Elena's turn to be surprised. "No, I didn't. Whatever made you decide to do a thing like that? It's all you've talked about since I've known you."

Maggie shrugged. "Like you said, there's more to life...."

For a moment Elena looked uncertain, then she relaxed with a smile. "Well, as long as you're happy. And I must say, I've never seen you look happier."

She turned and spread her arms expansively around the room. "This color is spectacular! It's like something from a magazine. I can't believe you didn't have a decorator pick it out for you."

"Well, actually, Chris—" Maggie bit off the word, then squared her shoulders determinedly. It wasn't as though Elena didn't know about Christopher, after all. She had nothing to be reserved about. "Christopher helped me pick it out," she finished, almost defiantly.

Elena turned slowly, a rather guarded expression on her face. "Christopher," she repeated. "The—er—ghost?"

Maggie nodded.

Elena cleared her throat and tried to look nonchalant. "Oh, is he still around?"

Maggie repressed a smile. "Constantly."

"Well. Imagine that." She gave a nervous little smile. "He's lasted longer than most of my boyfriends. You can't fault that kind of loyalty, I guess."

Elena looked uneasily around. "Is he—here? Now?"

Maggie couldn't help feeling sympathetic for her friend's discomfort. She nodded. "He's over there," she said gently. "By the door."

Elena turned with a jerky little movement toward the door, and Christopher bowed from the waist.

"Enchanté," he murmured.

Maggie could see the muscles in Elena's throat work as she swallowed. "I'm—not supposed to see him, am I?"

"No," Maggie sighed. "No one can see him but me."

"One must admire her poise," commented Christopher. "Please tell her I'm sorry we can't meet under more conducive circumstances."

Maggie glanced uncertainly at Christopher, then at Elena. She took a breath. "Christopher says he's sorry he can't meet you under more conducive circumstances."

"Oh." Elena looked at the door, looked back at Maggie, and then didn't seem to know where to look. She toyed with her earring and smoothed her hair. "Likewise, I'm sure," she murmured at last.

Then Elena cleared her throat and walked over to the gas heater, spreading her hands before the low flame as though to warm them. The moment was tense and uncomfortable, and Maggie looked helplessly at Christopher.

"This, I think," observed Christopher, "must be the test of a true friendship. Would it make it easier for you if I did something to draw attention to myself?"

"No," Maggie said quickly, and Elena turned, startled.

"I was—I was talking to Christopher," Maggie explained with an awkward lift of her hand.

"You talk to him," Elena repeated tonelessly. "And he talks back?"

Maggie felt a prickle of irritation. "Of course."

"All the time?"

"Of course, all the time. I told you that. I explained it all to you before...."

"I know you did." Elena turned back to the fireplace. She stretched her shoulders, as though shrugging off a burden—or adjusting to a new one—and her voice sounded deceptively casual as she asked, "Have you heard from Larry lately?"

"A couple of nights ago," Maggie answered carefully. She had an uneasy feeling something was going on in Elena's head that she did not quite like. "He's coming back next week."

"I find myself growing bored," announced Christopher, "as so often happens when that particular gentleman's name is mentioned. I think I will leave you two ladies to your girl talk."

Maggie turned quickly, but Christopher was gone.

"Do you know what you really need?" Elena said. Her voice was high and tight, and her smile a little false. "A nice sofa and a teapot, so we could cozy up for a little chat."

"Christopher's gone," Maggie said, hoping to put her friend at ease. "It makes me a little nervous, too, to know he's listening to every word. But you can relax now."

Elena did not appear to be entirely ready to relax. She cast one more uncertain look around the room. "Where does he, um, go?"

Maggie shrugged. "Nowhere, probably. Most of the time he's still around; I just can't see him. But sometimes he actually does turn off to me—he calls it resting—and because I can't tell the difference, it's easier to pretend he's really not here."

Elena stared at her for a long time, as though struggling to make sense of what Maggie had said. Maggie grinned and gestured to a stepstool in the corner that she had used for painting. "It may not be very cozy, but have a seat. Let's chat."

After a moment, Elena went over to the stool and sat down, arranging her skirts gracefully over her legs as she propped up her heels on the bottom step. Maggie folded a drop cloth on the floor and sat down beside her, wrapping her arms around her updrawn knees.

Elena shook her head a little, as though clearing away a daze. "It must be—hard for you, living with a ghost."

"It was at first," Maggie admitted. "I've always been such a loner, and you know how I hated anybody interfering in my work or my privacy. But now...I don't know. It's more than second nature. It's like he's the other half of me, and I can't remember what it was like when he wasn't here."

Maggie had not realized how good it would feel to put the experience into words nor how badly she had wanted to share it. When she had first told Elena about Christopher, it had been because she was uncertain and confused. Now it was like sharing good news; a personal triumph or a miracle, something too wonderful to keep to oneself.

Her voice softened, and a secret smile touched her lips as she went on, "Oh, Elena, you wouldn't believe what a difference he's made in my life. He makes me see everything differently, he's opened up my eyes to things I never even considered before. And God, he's fun to be with." She chuckled softly to herself. "Every day is an adventure with him. I never know what to expect next. And yet..." Her voice grew thoughtful as she tried to put it into words. "I've never known anyone I could trust as much as Christopher or confide in...I didn't think it was possible to ever be that close to anyone, you know? There aren't any secrets. There's nothing he doesn't understand about me, and he's always there for me. It's like..." And then she hesitated, because she couldn't say exactly what it was like. And she was, for some reason, embarrassed over having put such intensely personal feeling into words, even for Elena.

Maggie shrugged a little. "I guess you can't really know what it's like until it's happened to you."

Elena said, seeming to choose her words carefully. "He sounds perfect."

Maggie smiled. "He is."

Elena hesitated and then seemed to come to a decision. Maggie could see the tendons of her hands stretch as she clasped them tightly in her lap, and that made her uneasy.

"Maggie," Elena said, "I've got a confession to make." She lifted her eyes to Maggie's, and her expression was bravely determined. "I didn't come here today just to see your house. I came because I was worried about you. And because I talked to Larry last night and he asked me to check on you."

"Larry! What—"

"He's worried, too," Elena went on firmly. "He was afraid you were wearing yourself out with this house, and I was hoping it was just that simple."

"That's ridiculous! The two of you—"

"Oh, come on, Maggie! We had every right to be worried, and you know it. I've never known you to turn down a free meal in your life, and you've refused two dinner invitations this week alone. Nobody ever sees you anymore, you don't answer your phone... Now you tell me you've decided to forget your doctorate—"

"I didn't forget it. I've just postponed it."

Elena took a deep breath, as though needing the fortification. But her gaze did not waver. "I knew there was something wrong," she said quietly. "I just wasn't sure what it was. Now I know. You're in love with this ghost."

The silence in the room was as resounding as the echo after an explosion. Maggie in fact felt as though she had been knocked off her feet by something just as powerful and unexpected as an explosion. And for the longest time all she could do was stare at Elena.

"That's—that's the craziest thing I ever heard!" she managed at last, breathlessly. "In love—" Color rose to her cheeks in a rush, but she wasn't sure whether it was due to anger or dismay...or the embarrassment that comes when a secret truth is brought to light. "It's—it's absurd!"

"Is it?" returned Elena immediately. Now that the words had been spoken, her reticence seemed to have fled and her voice was forceful, her expression intense. "Have you been listening to yourself? Your Christopher—a combination of Lord Byron and Albert Einstein with a little Dr. Schweitzer thrown in for good measure. You've described the perfect fantasy man, and you've described him through the eyes of a lover!"

Maggie got to her feet, her eyes glittering. "I'm not listening to any more of this—"

"All right!" Elena threw up her hands in concession. "If not love, then obsession—either way it's not healthy, and you know it!"

Maggie clenched her fists tightly at her sides. "I thought you were my friend. I thought you believed me. I told you all this because I trusted you—"

"God, Maggie, I do believe you! That's the problem, don't you see?"

Elena got up and came over to Maggie, her face tight and anxious, but Maggie turned away. "You don't believe me," Maggie said coldly. "You think I've invented all this out of some psychotic need for—for I don't know what! I thought you knew me better than that, Elena. I thought I knew you better than that."

Elena was silent for a moment, and when she spoke again her voice sounded strained. "Maggie, I do believe you, as much as I can. I want to believe you. Just like—like I want to believe that there are healing forces in ordinary rocks that are waiting for us to discover, and like I want to believe that there's intelligent life on other planets, because it makes it easier to believe that there's intelligent life on this one.... And I want to believe that death isn't the end of life because everyone wants to believe that.... Maggie, please. I'm doing the best I can. Just listen to me for a minute, please?"

Maggie didn't want to. She didn't want to stand there and watch while the delicate fortress of her secret world was shattered by blunt stones of reason. She didn't want to hear any of this. *Christopher,* she thought desperately, *where are you? Make her stop this. Don't let her do this....*

But Christopher didn't come. Slowly, Maggie turned to face Elena.

"All right," she said quietly, "I'm listening."

Elena folded her hands against her lips and took a slow, steadying breath. "Maggie," she said after a moment, "you've always been...an escapist kind of person. It used to be that whenever things got too intense for you, especially relationship-wise, you'd hide behind your work. Now you're hiding behind something else. It doesn't matter whether Christopher is real or not, whether I believe in him or not. The fact is, you're using him to escape from the real world and . . . from things that used to be important to you. Can you at least admit that's a possibility?''

"You sound like a psychiatrist, Elena," Maggie said impatiently. "Give me a little more credit than that, okay?"

"All right." Elena lifted her palms in quick defense. "Okay, you're right. I hate people who play amateur shrink. But will you answer me this—how long do you expect it to go on?"

Maggie was a little taken aback and thoroughly uncertain for the first time since the conversation had begun. "What do you mean?"

"You—and Christopher. You've told me all these wonderful things about him, what he means to you and what he's done for you, and I don't doubt any of them for a minute, I honestly don't. But—is it going to be like this for the rest of your life? Maggie, you've cut yourself off from your friends and your work and even Larry—and I'll grant you, he may not be perfect, but at least he's alive. Are you going to shut yourself up with a ghost for the rest of your life?"

Maggie had no answer for that. She couldn't even begin to form one.

"What if you want to get married someday?" Elena persisted. "What about children? What about—what about giving a simple little dinner party? What are you going to say to your guests, 'this is my companion, Christopher, you'll have to pardon him, he's a little on the invisible side'? Maggie, you can't live forever without a social life!"

Maggie brought her hands to her hot cheeks, uncertain whether that hysterical tickle in the back of her throat was the urge to laugh or to cry. "Elena, stop it. You're being crazy—"

"What happens," Elena insisted, completely caught up in the speculation now, "when you grow old and he doesn't? How are you going to feel about your choices then? Okay, I know I'm talking crazy, but I'm just trying to make you see this thing like it is. You're letting it take over your whole life, and it can't go on forever."

"I can't predict the future," Maggie said, and even her muscles ached with the effort to control her voice. "I don't know the answer to any of your questions. They're stupid questions anyway, it's not like that—"

"All right then," Elena said calmly, "how about a not-so-stupid question. What about him? What's going to happen to him?"

Maggie only looked at her blankly.

"Maggie, you know this isn't right. You've got an earthbound spirit who shouldn't be here, and you don't even want to set him free."

Maggie shook her head, relieved at last to be able to get at least some kind of grip on the conversation. "We've talked about this before. Everything's not as simple as what you read in books, Elena, and who's to say what's right and wrong? Maybe he doesn't want to be free." But even as she spoke, she was aware of a hollowness to her words. She remembered the pain on Christopher's face as he described the torment of having and not having, of being trapped between two worlds.... No, it wasn't right. How long could she go on pretending it was?

But what was she supposed to do?

Elena shook her head, dismissing Maggie's last words with a simple breath of despair. "If only you knew why

he had returned and what was keeping him here...."
Then she looked at Maggie suddenly. "How did he
die?"

"I don't know." Maggie remembered the answers she
had gotten whenever she asked that question, ranging
from the absurd to the outright evasive. She added
thoughtfully, almost questioningly, "I'm not sure...he
knows."

"Then that's it!" Elena exclaimed in a low voice. "If
you could find out how he died, you'd have the key to
setting him free. And you have to do that, Maggie," she
added, her face creased with concern. "For his sake—
and yours."

Maggie didn't answer because she had no answer to
give. And for a long time after Elena had gone, she sat
on the floor, her head buried in her knees, waiting for
Christopher.

Chapter Twelve

IT WAS THE NEXT DAY before Maggie remembered the information Larry's secretary had gathered for her on the history of the house. Perhaps she had put it out of her mind until then because she suspected Cecile might have found something she had not...and perhaps it was something she didn't really want to know.

Cecile had, indeed, done her homework. There were copies of registry records, permits, titles and deeds. There was even a copy of the original land plat. And at the bottom of the file was the copy of a newspaper article: Local Architect Dies in Street Accident.

Maggie read it, reread it and read it again. With each reading it became more real to her, until finally it seemed the most important thing she had ever known. Christopher Durand had died on New Year's Eve, 1899, struck down by a motorcar as he crossed a street in Baltimore. No trumpets, no fanfare, no grand heroic gestures, just a mundane street accident. Mention of the house on Walnut Street was made, and according to his contemporaries he would be sorely missed.

The information did not materially change anything, of course. It wasn't as though she were surprised to learn of his death, after all. It was just that seeing it in print somehow made it so final...so real. A street accident. A stupid street accident.

She was sitting alone at the divider bar in her apartment kitchen with a cup of coffee. This was the time of

morning when she could generally count upon having a
few moments to herself; sometimes she teased Christopher about being a late riser. Now she wished she
weren't quite so alone.

She fingered the slick Xerox copy of the article and
tried to smile, but she was surprised to feel her throat
thicken with tears. "New Year's Eve, huh?" she muttered. "He was probably on his way to a party." And
then the tears rose and burned her eyes, and she whispered, "Only a few more hours, Christopher, and you
would have lived to see the twentieth century you love
so much...."

The phone shrilled beside her, and she quickly
scrubbed away her tears. She let the phone ring one
more time, until she could control her voice enough to
answer it.

It was Larry.

"Welcome back," she said, and even managed to
sound convincing. "Early flight, wasn't it?"

"Red-eye. I got in at six." He sounded tired but, as
always, warmly affectionate toward her. "It's good to
be home. Better to hear your voice."

"How was your trip?"

She didn't really want to know, and she was glad he
didn't want to tell her. "Dull and uneventful. I'll tell
you about it later. What I really want to know is—how
are you?"

She knew she should be upset with him for having
sent Elena to check up on her, but she couldn't be. Because he was right. Elena was right. She had to get herself together.

Christopher had said nothing to her about her conversation with Elena, but she suspected he had heard it
all. Maggie had thought of nothing else, and one thing

was clear: she couldn't let Christopher take over her life, as great as the temptation was. She had to start acting sensibly about this thing, get her priorities straight, remember that she lived in the real world with real people. And those people cared about her, just as much as Christopher did. They were as important to her—almost as important—as Christopher was. Surely she could find a way to juggle both parts of her <u>life and</u> make it work.

She said, "I'm fine, Larry. And I'm glad you're back."

"Did you think about us, like you promised?"

She tried not to hesitate too long. "Of course, I did. I'm...just not sure exactly what you wanted me to think about."

"We'll talk about that," he said, and his tone held the warmth of a tantalizing promise, "at length. But first I wanted to tell you—my folks have invited us to dinner tonight. You'll come?"

"Dinner?" That was a surprise. She had never met Larry's family; she couldn't imagine why they would suddenly want her to come to dinner. "With your family?"

"I want them to meet you," Larry said. "And I want you to meet them. It's about time, don't you think?"

"Well, I guess..."

"It's important to me, Maggie. And I hope, after we have our talk, it will be important to you."

Perhaps it was a stab of guilt brought about by Larry's natural tenderness and her own indifference; perhaps it was because of her newly formed resolution to get her life in order. But suddenly Maggie heard herself saying, "I'll tell you what. I'll cook. Bring your parents here."

Larry's shocked silence was predictable and almost made Maggie smile. "Honey—are you sure? I mean, you hate to entertain, and this is pretty short notice. I wouldn't want to put you out . . ."

"What's the matter, are you afraid of my cooking? Anybody can throw a few steaks and potatoes in the oven."

"No, I'm sure it'll be great, it's just so much work. After all, I invited you to dinner."

"I want to do this, Larry," Maggie assured him, and the amazing thing was, she meant it. "I really do."

There was a brief pause, and then Larry said softly, "You're great, sweetheart. Do you know how much I love you?"

It was a moment before Maggie could find the right half-playful, half-sincere tone of voice, "Seems you may have mentioned it once or twice." Then she added quickly, "Listen, Larry, you'd better get some rest, and I've got to get to work. Shall we say about seven? Is that too early?"

"Perfect."

"Great. I'll see you then." And then, because she was afraid that might have sounded a little cavalier, she added softly, "Welcome home again."

"Well, well." Christopher was standing beside her when she hung up the phone. "He certainly roped you into that one neatly, didn't he?"

Quickly, Maggie began stuffing the papers she had been reading back into the envelope. Christopher didn't appear to notice.

"I don't know what you're talking about. I volunteered."

"Whatever possessed you to do such a foolish thing?" he demanded.

At the moment that seemed like a very good question, and Maggie felt a wave of dismay sweep through her as she looked around the kitchen. The refrigerator, if she recalled correctly, contained half a pint of milk and two eggs, and the cupboards were equally bare. She would have to do the marketing from the ground up. And her apartment was a mess. She was in the middle of packing for the move, and half her possessions were in cardboard boxes stacked in closets. She would have to buy guest towels and probably extra glasses...maybe she should call a caterer. She had intended to spend the day at the house, painting the upstairs hall, but obviously that would have to wait.

"I don't know," Maggie admitted, running a hand distractedly through her hair. "I'm still trying to figure out why Larry invited me to dinner."

"I'll tell you why," Christopher said adamantly. "The man wants you to meet his parents to show you what a lovely family you could have. And you invited them here to show off what a perfect little wife you'd make."

Maggie stared at him in outright astonishment. "That's ridiculous!"

"He set it up perfectly," Christopher insisted shortly. "And you fell right into the trap. The King of Dullness is going to ask you to marry him!"

Maggie opened her mouth for an incredulous rebuttal, but fell silent. Christopher was probably right, and she must have known it all along. Everything about Larry's behavior lately had indicated such a decision was coming, and she had done nothing to discourage it....

She frowned uncomfortably and took her coffee cup to the sink. "So? That doesn't mean I have to say yes."

"I don't know how you could even consider such a thing."

Maggie stiffened and braced her hands against the sink. It seemed to require almost more courage than she possessed to turn and face Christopher. "I could consider it," she said quietly. "Why shouldn't I? Larry's good for me, he has been for a long time. We get along well. We have the same interests. We understand each other. He's just what I need," she told Christopher deliberately, "to keep my feet on the ground."

And there it was, the moment of truth between them, the issue they had been avoiding, separately and together, since Elena's visit. She saw recognition register in Christopher's eyes, and though she expected sarcasm, anger or even hurt, he merely smiled. It was a small, dry smile, but it contained more gentleness than bitterness.

"So that's it, then," he said softly. "I've pushed you into the arms of another man."

The morning light played upon the silky fall of his hair and caressed the planes of his face. The light in his eyes was tender and knowing, and the sound of his voice as soothing as an embrace. Maggie felt her chest constrict, just looking at him, and she wanted to turn away from the pain, the betrayal, the truth. But defiantly, courageously, she held her ground.

"Tell me," Christopher said, and his voice was deceptively casual, "why doesn't he know about me?"

Maggie swallowed hard. "I—you know why. I can't tell him. He wouldn't understand."

"Your friend Elena understands," Christopher insisted. "Perhaps not very well, but at least she tries. And she accepts you for it. Why don't you tell Larry about me?"

"Because it has nothing to do with him! He wouldn't be interested, he—"

"But I thought he understood you so well. I thought you had so much in common. How does he feel about dragons, Maggie, and fairy castles and crystal balls?"

"That's not the point—"

"Why don't you tell him about me, Maggie?"

"Because I can't!" she cried. Her face was hot, and her eyes were stinging, but she was certain it was not from tears. She clenched her fists and determinedly ignored the burning in her eyes. "I can't, okay? Because it's too confusing. Because you and he are from separate worlds, and I want to keep it that way!"

"And you prefer his world to mine?" Christopher demanded quietly. "You would condemn yourself to a life of mortgages and percentage rates and soulless practicalities? Is that what you want?"

Maggie's fingernails dug painfully into her palms, but her voice was amazingly steady. "Maybe," she said forcefully. "Maybe that is what I want. Little challenges, minor problems, things I can count on. Things I can understand. I've got to have a normal life, Christopher!"

"But you are not a normal person," he told her gently. "You are an extraordinary, magical person, with dreams you haven't even touched yet and the power to make those dreams come true."

"I'm a scientist!"

He looked at her for such a long, thoughtful moment that she wanted to cover her face, to shrink away from the awful, heartbreaking perception of his gaze. But she didn't.

Christopher said quietly, "I heard your friend Elena talking. I can't fault you for that, or her. She is in many ways very wise, in others, very wrong. But you haven't answered the most important question she asked you. Are you in love with me, Maggie?''

Maggie's fingers went to her lips as though to still the too quick, too truthful answer that leaped there. And then she had to turn away.

"No!" she whispered, and though it was little more than a gasp, the single word seemed to echo. She wrapped her arms around herself and refused to look at him. "No," she repeated more forcefully, but still the word sounded hollow and desperate. "I can't love you. You're a ghost, an earthbound spirit who shouldn't even be here—"

"The only one who's earthbound," Christopher said, "is you. And you will be forever unless you stop selling short your dreams. I should hate to see that happen, Maggie, love," he added softly, "but it remains, as always, your choice."

A SUBTLE TENSION CRACKLED throughout the apartment the remainder of the day, and the nervousness Maggie felt had to do with more than the strain of preparing a dinner party on short notice and the anticipation of meeting Larry's parents. Even when Christopher seemed to overcome his resentment of Larry long enough to volunteer to help Maggie with the menu and take an active interest in her preparations for the evening, the undercurrent of uneasiness remained. Maggie knew it was because she could not forget what Christopher had said. She could not pretend the volatile encounter between them this morning had not happened; she could not dismiss the turmoil his questions had generated inside her. And she knew she was being pushed, consistently and inevitably, toward making a choice. Though she rejected that moment with all her might, it remained lurking in the future like an iceberg hidden by the fog. The stormy course of her own confusion would eventually bring her to a collision.

As it turned out, she had nothing, technically, to worry about. The roast that Christopher had suggested instead of steaks was done to perfection, the salad was tossed, the asparagus tips were tender, and the cheesecake had been transferred from its bakery box to a cake plate in the refrigerator. Maggie allowed herself a touch of pride at her culinary accomplishments and decided that if it was this easy, she wouldn't mind giving dinner parties more often.

At precisely two minutes before seven, Christopher reappeared, breathtaking in a white dinner jacket with a small rosebud pinned to the lapel. Had anyone in the entire history of the world ever looked as good in a dinner jacket, Maggie wondered. How was it possible that any one man could be so handsome, so debonair, so perfectly suited to any environment, and how could she have failed to appreciate that fact for so long?

Maggie was so stunned by his appearance that she didn't have time to reprimand him for his presence. She hadn't counted on him being visible tonight, but she was foolish not to have done so. The doorbell rang, and as she hastily smoothed the waistband of her emerald taffeta skirt and the high collar of her white blouse, Christopher bowed deeply to her. She should have known then that mischief was afoot.

Larry's father was a big, distinguished looking man who, Maggie had heard Larry say at one time or another, was a corporate lawyer. His wife was petite and dark haired; in fact, in size and appearance, she very much resembled Maggie.

"How sweet," Christopher murmured as Maggie took the older woman's fur coat. "You can wear each other's clothes."

Maggie was a little taken aback herself by the resemblance, or she never would have risked replying to him. "A lot of men like women who look like their mothers," she whispered as she turned to hang the fur on the coatrack.

"Did you say something, hon?"

Larry was at her side, and Maggie smiled at him nervously. "You didn't tell me they were rich," she said in a careful undertone, watching the way his mother seemed to inspect her sofa before she sat down. "This is real mink."

Larry chuckled. "She earned it, believe me, putting up with Dad all these years."

"He looks a little like his father, too," Christopher commented. "Except the father has more hair."

"Well," Maggie said brightly, and perhaps a fraction too loudly, "Would anyone like some wine?"

Maggie could tell that Larry was as nervous about this meeting as she was, which didn't do much to put her at ease. Though she already regretted having undertaken the project, she was more determined than ever to make the evening perfect...mostly because Christopher, with a knowing twinkle in his eye, was watching with such interest.

"So," Larry's mother said when they were all settled in the living room with glasses of wine, "Larry tells me you're a teacher."

"A teacher," scoffed Christopher. "She makes it sound as though you're just passing time with fingerpaints until someone comes along to rescue you from all this."

"Actually," Maggie said, doing her best to ignore him, "I'm working on my doctorate in physics. I teach at the junior college to help pay expenses."

"My goodness, how ambitious." Mrs. Hanes lifted one delicately arched eyebrow. "I do admire women these days. It was all I could do to keep up with my three boys and try to be a proper hostess for Charlie's clients—which was quite a job, I do assure you. But I suppose you'll go right on working, even after you have a family. It's really amazing."

"And this is what you have to look forward to," Christopher muttered.

"Women do have more choices today, Mrs. Hanes," Maggie said carefully, and Larry took her hand, squeezing just a little too hard.

"Maggie's a brilliant woman, Mother," he said energetically. "And very talented. I'm very proud of her."

"What has he got to be proud of?" Christopher frowned. "He had nothing to do with it."

"Still, certain problems do arise with career women, dear. Now, I know it's old-fashioned, but—"

"Doesn't her husband ever talk?" Christopher said. "I'd like to see where his son got his scintillating personality."

Larry's father took a sip of wine and set the glass down. Maggie wished she had asked for a more expensive brand.

"Maybe he'd like to watch some television." Christopher reached for the remote control on the end table beside Maggie.

Maggie lunged for the device and snatched it from him, but not before almost upsetting a lamp, and not before the television blared out a football game. Quickly she fumbled for the button that would turn the television off and met the startled gazes of her three guests.

"Where's your cat, Maggie?" Larry asked.

"What cat?" she repeated breathlessly.

There was a beat of silence, then Larry turned to his mother with a nervous laugh. "Maggie has the cleverest cat . . ."

"Excuse me." Maggie stood abruptly. "I have to check the roast."

She slammed open the oven door and covered the sound of her voice with a great deal of rattling of pans and utensils. "How dare you!" she hissed furiously to Christopher. "What do you think you're doing—"

"Entertaining your guests," replied Christopher blandly, "as a good host should."

"I don't need your snide comments, and I certainly don't need your help!" Maggie flung open the refrigerator door and took out the salad. "You're trying to rattle me, and you're doing it on purpose—"

Christopher stepped gracefully out of her way as she swung around and set the salad on the counter. "I'm doing no such thing. And my comments are not snide, they're a mere statement of fact—"

"In your opinion!"

"Those people are insufferable, which is hardly surprising considering—"

"You're the one who's being insufferable!" She began to transfer the salad, hastily and somewhat sloppily, into bowls. "This is none of your business, this is my party—"

"Maggie, honestly." His tone was impatient as he took down the meat platter from an overhead shelf. Maggie grabbed it from him quickly. "You can't say that you want to spend the rest of your life with people like that, eventually turning into one of them—''

"I'm the one who'll decide what to do with the rest of my life!"

"Maggie?"

The sound of Larry's voice startled her, and she whirled, almost dropping the platter. His face was concerned, and his eyes held a trace of displeasure as he came toward her. "What's going on in here?" he kept his voice carefully low. "What are you muttering about? We can hear you all the way to the living room."

Maggie swallowed hard, clutching the platter to her chest defensively. "I'm sorry, Larry, I guess I'm a little frazzled."

Larry smiled and put a sympathetic arm around her shoulders. "There's nothing to be nervous about, you know. They may be a little stuffy, but they're just people, and probably as nervous as we are."

Maggie looked anxiously over his shoulder toward the living room. "I don't think your father likes me."

"Nonsense." Larry gave her shoulders a reassuring squeeze. "How could he not like you?"

"He hasn't said a word."

"He isn't very good at social small talk."

"If you don't serve this roast immediately it will be ruined," Christopher observed, testing the meat with a fork.

Maggie quickly stepped away from Larry, putting herself between him and the roast and hoping his parents didn't turn suddenly and see a fork floating in the air. "If I don't serve the roast now, it will be ruined," she blurted, a little desperately.

"It's okay." Larry's expression was partly amused, partly puzzled at her overreaction. "Don't get so uptight. Everything will just fine, I'm sure." He cast an uncertain eye at the lettuce scattered over the counter and added, "Do you need any help?"

"No thanks. Just—go entertain your folks for a minute while I get things on the table." Suddenly the only thing she could think of was to get this dinner over with, and quickly. She could feel disaster hovering in the air.

As soon as Larry turned his back, she snatched the fork from Christopher and transferred the meat to the platter. She got the food on the table with unseemly haste, and when she went to announce dinner, she overheard Larry's father commenting, "She seems a little strange to me, son. You know there are a lot of drugs on college campuses these days...."

Maggie's color rose angrily, and Christopher said, "He thinks you're strange? He should take a good look in the mirror."

She announced dinner in her most gracious tone, but she could see Christopher was seething. And even though her nerves were frayed and she had never been more impatient with Christopher in her life, she could not deny a certain amount of gratitude for his support. She had noticed that Larry had not exactly leaped to her defense before his father.

"It looks lovely, dear," Larry's mother remarked as she was seated. "Who would think a busy girl like you would have the time to cook?"

"I do my best," Maggie murmured tightly. Christopher was right. They were insufferable. But Larry hadn't had anything to do with choosing his parents, and Maggie certainly didn't need Christopher to point out other people's shortcomings. If only she could get through this evening....

"Physics, huh?" pronounced Larry's father abruptly. He fixed Maggie with a piercing stare. "Tell me, what is the world of science offering our bright young people today?"

Maggie opened her mouth to reply, but Larry's mother interrupted fatuously, "A scientist, my word! She hardly looks old enough to be out of high school, does she, dear?" She turned to Maggie. "Were you a prodigy?"

Christopher said, "Someone should carve the roast."

Maggie snatched the carving tools off the platter before he could reach for them and thrust them at Larry so forcefully that he flinched. "Would you carve the roast?" she asked quickly.

Christopher gave her an odd, rather amused look and stepped away from the table. He leaned against the wall with his arms and ankles crossed, as though displaying his intention not to interfere. Maggie somehow found his silent observation more disconcerting than his intrusion.

Larry took the tools from her carefully, turning the blade of the knife away from him, and his father chuckled gruffly. "Good thing she didn't decide to become a surgeon, eh, son? I always say there's nothing more dangerous than a woman with a knife in her hand."

Larry smiled weakly, but the look he gave Maggie was filled with restrained impatience. He was as close to losing his temper as Maggie had ever seen him.

Avoiding his eyes, Maggie picked up the bread basket and hastily passed it to his mother. *It's only a dinner party,* she thought, transferring some of her annoyance with Christopher to Larry. *Why is he being so touchy?*

Larry's mother refused the bread basket with a demure, "No, dear, my figure. At your age one doesn't have to worry, I'm sure, but... How old are you, if you don't mind my asking?"

Larry gave an overloud laugh and winked broadly at his mother. "Past the age of consent, Mother," he said. "I haven't robbed the cradle since I was a teenager."

No one laughed, and Maggie was embarrassed. Had Larry always been this stiff and boorish, or was it only his parents who made him act this way? Could she be seeing a side of him she'd never known before?

Dinner dragged on; conversation dragged on. Larry's father drank too much wine. Larry's mother picked at her food and, when pressed, confessed that the roast might be just a touch dry. Maggie could not remember spending a more strained or miserable evening in her life.

Christopher stood like a silent accusation in the corner of the room, tall, elegant, beautiful. Occasionally Maggie would glance at him, as though for reassurance, but he was impassive. He did not have to say anything; his thoughts echoed like low thunder through the room: *Is this what you want for yourself, Maggie? Is this how you've always pictured yourself living? Is this what you want to become—dull, staid, humorless? Do you want to spend the rest of your life watching Larry turn into his father and you into his mother? Maggie, what can you be thinking of?* Or perhaps those weren't Christopher's thoughts at all; perhaps they were her own.

Sitting at that dinner table, forcing herself to be nice to people she could not convince herself she liked, Maggie felt like an impostor. She kept waiting for Christopher to do something, say something—anything—to relieve the awful tedium of the evening. And when he didn't, the expectation only wound her nerves to the snapping point. Snatches of their conversation that morning kept rolling through her head, and though she tried to blot them out, she couldn't.

It was all Christopher's fault. If only he hadn't put doubts into her mind about Larry, if only he hadn't forced her to see through his eyes. If only he had never appeared and made her see how exciting life could be....

At last Maggie got up to serve dessert, and the evening was almost over. As she was taking her seat again, Larry stood, raising his wineglass.

"I'd like to propose a toast," he said. Obediently, the others gave him their attention, and he turned to Maggie. "To the gracious hospitality of Maggie Castle, a charming hostess, an excellent cook and, I hope—" The smile he gave her was tender and affectionate, and Maggie should have known what was coming next. Amazingly, she didn't. "—My future wife."

There was a small choked sound from Larry's mother, and his father muttered dryly, "Now wasn't that a surprise?" Maggie simply sat there feeling stunned and dismayed as the evening went from bad to worse.

Larry looked down at her, still smiling warmly, and prompted, "Well, Maggie?" There seemed to be no doubt in his mind of her answer, and suddenly she knew he had staged all of this, thinking that all she needed was a public declaration of his intent to prompt a commitment. And maybe he was right. What more could she ask for? He had proposed marriage in front of his parents. He was serious, he was committed, he had left no room for argument or debate. All that was lacking was her answer.

She cast a desperate glance toward Christopher, but he merely raised one eyebrow slightly and said nothing. She jerked her eyes away, her hands tightening in her lap. This was what she wanted, wasn't it? Reality, solidity, an ordinary man in human form who wanted only to love her for the rest of her life.

Larry repeated, "Maggie?"

Maggie said, "No."

The word was very soft, but there was no way it could have been overlooked in the silence that suddenly hung over the table. The tension in the room was so thick it practically hummed. Maggie looked up at Larry, and she repeated, more clearly, "No. I'm sorry, Larry, but I can't marry you."

The astonishment on his face was almost comical. He looked self-consciously at his father, then back at Maggie, and a flush of color appeared on his cheeks. He stammered for a moment and then managed, "You're just surprised. Caught off guard. You need more time to think—"

"No!" Maggie crumpled up her napkin and placed it on the table. His humiliation became her own and that, in combination with the accumulated strain of the evening, pushed Maggie to her breaking point. "I'm sorry you're embarrassed, and I'm sorry you're disappointed, but you shouldn't have done this. I don't want to marry you. I can't marry you. I don't need any more time to think. I've made my decision, and that's that."

"But Maggie, we had an understanding—"

"You never understood me!" she cried, and got to her feet. "You never even listened to me! Do you think I want to spend the rest of my life like this?" She made a gesture that included the dinner table and his parents, and he looked confused. "Do you think I want to turn into somebody who only cares about mink coats and intimate little dinner parties and whether the roast is too dry? That's not me, Larry, and if you knew me at all you'd understand that!''

"Well, I never!" Larry's mother exclaimed.

Larry said stiffly, "There's no reason to raise your voice, Maggie."

"I can raise my voice if I want to! This is still my house, isn't it?" She couldn't believe the sound of her own voice, she couldn't believe she was being so childish, and she couldn't believe how quickly her control was slipping away. But neither could she stop. All she wanted was for this horrible evening to be over.

"You shouldn't have done this, Larry," she repeated angrily. "You shouldn't have brought your parents here, and you shouldn't have proposed marriage, and you shouldn't have assumed what my answer would be. Maybe you're seeing another side of me tonight, but I've seen another side of you, and I'm not sure I like it."

Larry put his glass on the table and reached out as though to take her arms, but Maggie brushed his hands away. "You can't control me, Larry," she said stiffly. "Are you ever going to learn that?"

"We should talk . . ."

"No." She took a breath and looked away. "I think—you should all go home now. I'd like to be alone."

Larry's father commented, "Well, I guess that's clear enough." And he stood.

Larry hesitated, then turned apologetically to his parents, "It seems Maggie isn't feeling well. . . ."

His mother murmured, "Yes, I feel a headache coming on myself."

Maggie turned away, hating herself and what she had done, wanting to apologize but unable to bring herself to do so. The sounds of the Haneses' leave-taking echoed around her, and she thought she heard Larry's mother murmur something about "a pleasant evening." And then Larry stood before her.

His face was stunned, and his eyes were hurt. He said quietly, "I'll call you." There was a plea behind the words.

Maggie said tiredly, "No. Don't. There's no point.'

He stood there for a moment, looking uncertain, but his parents were waiting. He walked away, and in a moment the door closed behind them.

Chapter Thirteen

MAGGIE HUGGED HER ELBOWS so tightly they hurt. She could feel the muscles straining, but no amount of force could hold back the raging turmoil of emotions that was seething and writhing inside her. She said in a very low voice "Are you happy now?"

"Yes," Christopher replied calmly. "I am. You did the right thing, just as I knew you would. And now that you're rid of him, you and I can get on with our lives."

She whirled on him, incredulity and outrage making her voice shrill. "Our lives? What lives? We have no lives, Christopher! All we have is you interfering and manipulating and trying to ruin what's left of my life every chance you get!"

"I didn't turn your suitor away," he reminded her. "You did."

"But I never would have if you hadn't interfered! If you hadn't kept criticizing and needling and telling me what I wanted...." *Making me see the truth,* a small voice echoed, but she refused to listen. "Maybe you don't know what I want any more than Larry does!"

He said gently, "Everything I've done has been for you."

But Maggie didn't want to hear that. She was helpless and confused and angry with herself and her own uncertainty. There was nothing for her to do but take that anger out on Christopher. "You've done nothing for me!" she cried. "All you've done is act like a spoiled, jealous child, and nothing matters except what you want! Well, I won't have it anymore, do you hear me? I won't have it!''

He took a step toward her, his voice soothing. ''Maggie, be reasonable....''

But it was too much. The accumulated tensions, despair and frustrations of the past months congealed and sharpened into a fine edge, and Maggie was past the point of reason.

''No!'' she said forcefully, and he stopped his approach. She pressed her hands together tightly, restraining wild emotion by force of will, and she repeated powerfully, ''No. I'm not going to listen to your pretty words anymore, and I'm not going to be taken in by your charm. I've had enough, do you understand that? This is my life, and I've got a right to live it!''

There might have been a flash of hurt in his eyes, but she was too far gone to notice or even care. ''Maggie,'' he said softly, ''you don't mean that. You know I'd never do anything to hurt you.''

''But you are hurting me! You're hurting me every minute you stay here, and I don't think you even care. You're only using me to stay connected to a life that isn't yours anymore, and you're ruining mine in the process. And you're so selfish, you don't even see it!''

''That's not true, Maggie,'' he said hoarsely, and, had she been even a fraction more rational, the pain in his eyes would have stopped her.

But Maggie was far beyond rationality. ''You're dead, Christopher,'' she said harshly, ''and you're just too stubborn—or too selfish—to admit it! There's no place for you in my life, there's no future or hope or point!''

''Maggie, don't do this...''

"I have to!" she cried. She could feel the fine web of emotional stability begin to shatter, allowing the raw edges of pain and despair to slice through. She buried her face briefly in her hands, but she couldn't hide from the truth. She looked at him helplessly, desperately. "Christopher, it isn't working, don't you see that? It can never work for us, it's hopeless, and it's destroying me! I can't live like this. I wasn't meant to live like this. I keep trying to make it all right, but I can't! God, it isn't fair! You can't ask me to do this any longer!"

Even as she spoke she wanted to stop; the words tore through her as though they had a separate will of their own, and they left a path of searing pain in their wake—pain that was reflected on Christopher's face, pain that ran like the jagged edge of a knife through Maggie's soul. But she couldn't stop. No power on earth could have made her stop.

"You're dead!" she cried. "Do you understand that? It's time for you to go away! You died beneath the wheels of an automobile in Baltimore on New Year's Eve, 1899, and nothing is going to change that, not ever! Your time is over, and you can't have it back!"

Christopher's face was carved into immobile lines of shock and disbelief, his eyes were dark with denial and the gathering thunderclouds of anger. He said, "No." Then, more forcefully, "No, that's not the way it happened at all! I remember distinctly—"

"You don't remember at all!" Horror battered Maggie like waves pounding against the shore, horror at what she had said, at what she was doing, at what she could not stop or take back. But her head was roaring, and her fists were clenched, and she could not hold back the words. As hard as she tried, she couldn't....

"As long as you don't remember you can pretend it didn't happen, but it did, Christopher! It's over!"

"Noooo!"

The cry echoed throughout the room, blue-white fury and flashing denial. Instinctively Maggie smothered a cry, her hands going to her face, but even as the echoes died away, the rage that tore at his face turned to anguish, and he cried again, "No!" as the reel of memory began to unwind.

It was agonizing to watch. Maggie wanted to turn her face away, to cry out against it, to somehow turn back time and destroy the monster of remembrance that she had unleashed. The pain in Christopher's eyes seemed to reach out and smother her as he whispered, "It was snowing. I was walking to the station. I was going home. I was thinking..." And suddenly the dull shock of recollection in his tone erupted into raw despair and he cried, "Oh, God, Maggie, it wasn't fair! I wasn't finished yet, I was waiting—I was waiting for you, Maggie! But I never knew you, I never loved you.... Maggie, why weren't you there?"

With a sob she stumbled toward him, reaching for him. She heard his muffled cry, and she was swept into an embrace of heat and color and desperate, desperate need. She clung to him, and his strength enfolded her tightly, muscles and flesh and roaring pulse. Yet her body was a distant thing of which she was hardly aware because her soul was flooded with Christopher, filled with Christopher... And truth like a river rushed through her, washing her clean and leaving her crying out for more.

Christopher. Since time began it had been Christopher, the lost part of her seeking its own. For every man there was a woman; for every woman, a man she was destined to love. Christopher was her destiny, yet through some accident of time she had missed him. He had lived and died loving her without knowing her, and through the decades he had waited for her, just as some deeply buried part of herself had been kept secret and alone all these years, waiting for him. But she hadn't known. All this time she had been alone, and she had never known it was Christopher for whom she waited. How could she not have known? Why had it taken so long for her to understand, and why must she understand now... when it was too late?

For the brilliant surge of light and color that swirled through her with his touch began to fade and grow dull with despair. She could no longer feel him. She tried to open her eyes, but she couldn't. She tried to cry out, but she had no voice. And all she could feel from him was resignation and sorrow. Unbearable sorrow.

"I have found you, love," he whispered. "Perhaps that was all I was meant to do."

She could feel him slipping away. She struggled against it; tried to scream, but the only sound was a silent echo inside her head. *I'm sorry, I'm sorry.... Please no, not now, don't do this...*

"I have had my life," he said softly, "and now I give you back yours."

Struggling frantically, she opened her eyes, and she saw him... but it wasn't really him. There was only a faint, shimmering outline of the form he once had been, sad and empty, like a memory fading with time.

"Goodbye, Maggie...."

"Christopher!" Then she had her voice; frantically she cried out for him, she stumbled toward him. "Christopher, no...."

She reached out for him, but grasped only air.

THREE DAYS LATER, MAGGIE SAT in the window booth of a small restaurant, watching the first snow of the season swirl through the air.

"It's pretty, isn't it?" Larry said gently, and Maggie managed to smile.

"Snow always makes everything seem so...new."

Larry had called every day since the dinner party. It had taken this long for Maggie to gather the courage to face him...to face herself. The tattered shreds of her life were slowly beginning to fall into place, and it was time she took control again. She had to adjust, to get her priorities straight. Christopher was gone. It was over. And she was empty.

Larry reached across the table and covered her hand with his. "I guess you know what I want to say. Honey, I'm sorry."

The flash of surprise she felt was the first real emotion she had experienced in days. "You're sorry? I'm the one who acted like a crazed thing in front of your parents. I embarrassed you and them and myself...."

The tightening of his hand on hers stopped her. "I had no right to put you on the spot like I did. I should have been more sensitive, and you were right to be upset, Maggie," he said earnestly. "If there's a problem, no matter what it is, we can work it out together. I'm not going to desert you."

Far deep inside her the part of her heart that wasn't frozen stirred with amazement. "Even after that—that display, you would still..."

"I want you to be my wife, Maggie," he said simply. "I made up my mind to that a long time ago. And that means for better or worse."

Maggie looked at him for a long time, wondering. And then she said softly, "I don't think I ever appreciated before what a wonderful man you are."

He smiled. "Does that mean your answer is yes?"

It should have been so simple. Larry was a wonderful man. His loyalty had been put to the ultimate test, and still he came through for her. He was solid, responsible and unshakable. What more could any woman ask?

How strange it was. Before Christopher, she had felt nothing, missed nothing. She had been content to live her life alone. But Christopher had shown her the joy of sharing, of being involved, of caring, deeply and intensely, for someone other than herself; of being a part of someone else's life. Now he was gone, but the need was still there. And Larry was offering to fill it.

She had what she wanted. She had her life back and a chance to live it in a normal, utterly pragmatic way. Small challenges, small triumphs, small dreams. Here was a man who was offering her everything she needed . . . except one.

She said thoughtfully, "Let me ask you something, Larry."

He stroked her thumb affectionately. "Anything."

"How do you feel about dragons?"

He blinked, and she thought she sensed a small stiffening. "What?"

But she didn't really need an answer. Gently, she clasped his hand in both of hers, and she said, "You'd make a wonderful husband, Larry. There's a part of me that wishes, more than anything in the world, that you could be my husband." She saw his protest rising, and she continued firmly and as gently as she could, "But I don't love you, Larry. And living in a marriage without love would be worse than—'' and she had to smile, briefly, wistfully, at her own choice of words ''—living with a ghost.''

She stood and came around the table to brush his cheek with a kiss. ''Here's the thing,'' she said softly. ''There's a woman for every man, just one person you were meant to love forever. There's someone out there for you, Larry. Your job is to find her, even if it takes a lifetime....'' She straightened up, gazing out the window at the falling snow, ''Or more.''

ON DECEMBER 10, MAGGIE MOVED into her house. She had thought it would be hard, that the sorrow would overwhelm her, that the memories would suffocate her and that, in the end, she would not be able to live there at all. In fact, it was just the opposite.

The corridors were filled with the resonance of Christopher, the walls exuded his presence, every nail and bolt shone softly with the pride of his care. This was the house he had built for her. Here he had lived, here he had waited, and here he would always be, if only in her memory. How could she ever live anywhere else?

A great deal of work remained to be done. The upstairs bath was a clutter of exposed pipes and broken tiles. All the bedrooms except one were closed off and would remain so until she had time to tackle them, one by one. The kitchen was only half painted, and the floor was covered with a tarp, awaiting the installation of new linoleum. But a big easy chair was drawn up before the fireplace in the library, and a gaily decorated Christmas tree was placed before the window in the parlor. Every piece of furniture in the secret room had been cleaned and polished until it shone. Maggie had not sold the Paul Revere cup, and she never would. Everything that had been Christopher's was just as he had left it, but soon her possessions would mingle with his, and when she went in there she would always be connected to him. The room would belong to both of them, just as he had intended it should.

There was still an emptiness inside her that nothing could fill, and there always would be. But, day by day, it was getting easier to bear. Because of Christopher she was different, she was stronger. She would never be sorry for what he had given her.

She was in the foyer, hanging a mirror. The bright winter's sun streamed through the uncurtained windows and bounced off the deep purple facets of the amethyst crystal—a gift from Elena—displayed on a small marble table opposite the mirror. Perhaps the stone didn't possess the magical properties Elena claimed, but it did brighten up the room. With the mirror and the glass-shelved display case that housed Maggie's collection of mystical figures, the foyer seemed flooded with light.

Maggie moved back to survey her work and tried to ignore the stab of emotion she felt when she recalled how she had vowed never to hang a mirror in this house. Things like that didn't matter anymore. And they mattered too much.

She stepped forward, helplessly drawn to the display case and the two dragons frozen in combat on the top shelf. Pendrake and Ulyssia. She picked up the figurine and cradled it to her cheek, and a wave of longing so intense swept her that her chest actually ached from it.

"Oh, Christopher," she whispered. "I do love you. I have loved you forever...."

A voice said softly behind her, "I have waited an eternity to hear you say those words."

Her heart stopped. Everything inside her stopped. She looked up, and there was a figure reflected beside hers in the mirror. She whirled, but it was no illusion.

"Christopher!"

The sunlight gleamed on the soft sweep of his hair and sparkled in his eyes. She could see the gentle shadings and highlights of his flesh. She wanted to touch him, to assure her other senses that what she saw was real. She even took a joyous, victorious step forward to do so, but stopped short, confusion and uncertainty battering her.

He smiled. "I always told you you had the power to make dreams come true," he said tenderly. "And love is the greatest power of all, isn't it?"

She was trembling all over. She could hardly get her breath. The small dragon figurine slipped from her fingers and landed with a harmless thud on the floor at her feet. "But how...? I thought..."

And suddenly she stopped and whirled toward the mirror. Her hand flew to her throat. "I can see you! I can see you in the mirror!"

The reflection next to hers took on a small, puzzled frown. "Shouldn't you be able to?"

"No!" she cried, and a wonderful, incredible possibility began to form within her. It was too incredulous to be real, too much to hope for.... Yet her face was flooded with color, her eyes shone with expectation and certainty, and when she turned back to him she knew... against all that was reasonable or possible or allowable in the world of science or metaphysics, she knew.

She reached out her hand, and he stretched his toward her. Their fingers met and entwined—warm flesh, solid bone, the strength and surety of a human touch...

"You're real," she whispered. "You have a body...." She closed her other hand around the muscles of his arm, pressed it against the lean, solid flesh of his chest. She felt the heartbeat and the breath. She looked up at him, glowing, ecstatic, helpless in the thrall of a miracle. "Christopher, you've come back to me, and you're real, you're here and you're alive...."

"Yes," he said slowly, and the bewilderment in his eyes gave over to gradually expanding joy and amazement. "I am."

He lifted his hands to her face, cupping it tentatively at first, then more certainly. His eyes took on a glow, and his own face was tinged with color as delight and wonder suffused him. "Maggie, your skin—so soft, softer than I ever imagined it would be... Your hair..." His eyes flashed with light and wonder as he ran his fingers through her curls, and words seemed to fail him as he let his hands traverse the planes of her face and the curve of her throat, pausing to press his fingertips against the frantic pulse that beat there. "Maggie, the sensation...I can feel you, love, I can touch you...."

She wanted to laugh; she wanted to cry. She ran her hands greedily over his arms and the warm flesh of his neck. And the only sound she could make was a broken whisper, "It can't be. It's impossible. How can it be?"

"Always you question the impossible!" His eyes snapped with unadulterated happiness and a kind of joyous hunger that was mirrored in thrills of excitement throughout her body as he touched her. "My God, Maggie, what does it matter how? It has happened. I'm here with you, and I will be always. Do you really care why?''

No, she didn't care. Where love was deep enough, and strong enough, anything was possible. Wonder, reverence and a joy so deep that a thousand lifetimes could not contain it swelled up inside of Maggie, and the only expression she knew was in laughter—sweet, rapturous, all-delighting laughter.

"Oh, Christopher, it doesn't matter! Nothing matters except this." She clutched his hands tightly, loving the feel of his fingers tightening on hers, his warmth going through her—human warmth, sexual warmth, the warmth of the man she loved. "It's not over! You've come back to me. We have our life now, the one we were always meant to have. Our life together!''

In his eyes was the same wondrous light that she felt washing through every cell and fiber of her body, yet a shadow of uncertainty crossed his face with her words. "How strange," he murmured. "Everything is— somewhat confused. Only a moment ago I seemed to know, but now I'm not sure how this happened. I don't remember..."

She caught her breath, searching his face. "Don't you remember how we met? How you waited for me all those years, how you lived before...?"

"I remember you," he assured her quickly, and there was no mistaking the love that surged through his eyes and the grip of his hands on hers. "It seems I remember you forever. Even beyond what I know, you were always there. And I remember our time together, the apartment where you lived and the things we said and felt.... And I remember this house."

He looked around, and the shadows of confusion began to trouble his eyes again. "It seems there was a time before, but the details are blurred, and even as I speak, the memory is fading...." Then he looked at her and smiled. He lifted his hand to her hair, and as he stroked her curls, letting each separate tendril wrap itself around his fingers and then loosen again, the disturbance in his expression faded. All that remained was an all-absorbing pleasure. "I suppose it would be rather inconvenient to remember one life while trying to live another, wouldn't it?"

"Oh, Christopher!"

She was in his arms, his mouth covering hers, and she tasted him. She felt the surge of his strength and his arms enfolding her. His thighs pressed into hers, his chest crushed her breasts, and the wave of sheer sexual desire that swept through her was electrifying, dizzying, ferocious in its demand and yet...soothing. For there was time. Plenty of time.

When the kiss was ended, still they held each other, hungry yet content, sated yet needing. Maggie listened to the pounding of his heart, treasured the whisper of his breath. She lifted her hands and cupped his face, and looked into his eyes for a very long time.

"Welcome home," she whispered.

He smiled, and bending to slip one arm beneath her knees, he swept her off her feet. "Yes, love," he said. He turned and began to mount the stairs. "Welcome home."

Epilogue

MORNING SUN DAPPLED Maggie's cheek and mixed with memories of the night. Dreams of Christopher, heat and darkness and searing passion; lean, long muscles, feathery touches, bodies straining and merging... But not dreams. Christopher was here and real, and this time Maggie had not imagined it... had she? *Oh, God,* she thought in sudden desperation, *Don't let it be a dream....*

For a moment she lay there, almost afraid to open her eyes. Then the sound came to her...soft breathing. Her hand crept out, and she felt warmth and solid flesh, the length of a man's forearm lightly covered with hair. Christopher. Her soul practically sighed the word. *Christopher.*

She opened her eyes and met his gaze, gentle, dark and beautiful. His head left an indentation in the pillow next to her, and his hair was tousled. Wonderingly, she touched the bristly stubble on his chin, and he smiled. Wordlessly she went into his arms.

His scent was intoxicating—warmth and musk and morning sunshine. Wholly male, wholly real. The contours of his body she had come to know so well during the night were new to her today, the planes and angles, the softness and the strength. For an endless moment Maggie let the sensation fill her, his body pressed close to hers, enfolding hers, his scent, his heat, the texture of his hair and the beat of his heart. She wanted to hold him forever.

His lips brushed her hair, and she felt the curve of his smile against her ear. "I smell coffee," he said.

Maggie laughed. "It's the automatic coffee maker, remember? Last night, when we went to the kitchen..."

"I remember the kitchen well," he murmured, and Maggie felt her cheeks grow warm. Every moment had its memory of insatiable passion, of bodies coming together in greed and wonder, unable to be parted for even the space of time it took to prepare a meal. The coffee maker had been set, but dinner had been forgotten last night. And as the details of what they had shared in the kitchen swept over her, Maggie felt a giddy surge of anticipation for the days and years of discovery that lay ahead of them.

Christopher, as perfectly attuned to her as he had always been, moved his hand over the curve of her hip in a gentle, sweeping caress that was certain to rekindle the embers of desire. But some instinct within Maggie warned against being too greedy too soon, against allowing herself to drown in the delirium of passion to the exclusion of all else. Reluctantly, she moved away kissing his cheek. "I'll get the coffee," she said.

His hand trailed upward to her waist, then linked with hers. The persuasion in his eyes was hard to resist. "Do you have to go this very moment?"

Determinedly, Maggie reached for the robe that hung on the bedpost and slipped it on, standing. "I have to leave you sometime," she said reasonably, though there was nothing in the world she wanted to do more than to crawl back in his arms and spend the rest of her life there. "If I don't, how will I know you'll still be here when I get back? How will I know you're not just a figment of my imagination?''

Christopher plumped up the pillow and leaned back with his arms crossed behind his head, smiling. "I'm not a figment of your imagination," he assured her. "I'll be here when you get back."

Nonetheless, Maggie hurried and was almost breathless when she returned to the bedroom with two mugs of coffee, a pitcher of cream and a bowl of sugar on a tray. Christopher was still there, sitting cross-legged on the bed, dressed in the pair of trousers he had worn when she had first seen him yesterday. His chest was bare, and her eyes lingered in renewed wonder over the definition of muscles and the pattern of dark hair. There were so many things she had never known about him, never even imagined about him, and each of them was a different kind of miracle.

She said, coming forward, "I didn't know if you took cream and sugar, so I brought both."

He took a cup of coffee from the tray. "Funny. I don't know, either."

"Christopher..." She set the tray on the bedside table and took her own coffee cup, sitting beside him on the bed. "Don't you remember anything about your former life?"

He shook his head. "My memory begins with the day I met you, here in this house."

"Do you remember being..." She couldn't say the word.

"Discarnate?" He smiled. "In a way. That is, I know I was, but I don't remember what it felt like. Odd, isn't it?"

"Yes," Maggie said softly. "Odd."

She reached out and touched his leg, letting her fingers linger against the scratchy material. "These feel like wool," she said. She looked at them. "Where did they come from? How can wool just materialize out of thin air?" Of all the questions and impossibilities that confronted her, that seemed like the simplest one to verbalize. Or perhaps it was simply a place to start. "Christopher, how did any of this happen?"

"Perhaps," he speculated thoughtfully, "some form of transmutation of matter?"

She shook her head. "Impossible. There's no proof of anything of the sort, not even an acceptable theory—"

"And the first law of science," Christopher retorted, "is that there is no such thing as the unknown. Only truths we haven't discovered yet."

"You can't just ignore the laws of physics—"

"Nor can you deny the fact that those laws have just been unmistakably broken."

Maggie opened her mouth for rebuttal and then stopped. She saw the intensity in his eyes as he paused with the coffee cup halfway to his lips. She saw the workings of his quick agile mind preparing his argument. She thought of the years of lively debate that lay ahead of them, and she laughed out loud in delight. "Will you always argue for the sake of argument?" she challenged him.

"As long as I'm able," he replied, his eyes twinkling. "Come here." He extended his arm for her, and she moved to snuggle against his chest.

He sipped his coffee and made a face. "I think I take cream and sugar."

"I was just getting comfortable."

"You're closer to the table."

"In the twentieth century, women are not slaves to men's commands."

"You're still closer."

Pretending reluctance, Maggie left the circle of his arm to reach for the tray. But her movement jostled the bed, and Christopher jerked back with an exclamation as coffee spilled on his hand.

"Are you burned?" Maggie bent in quick concern to examine his hand, were a faint pink spot was rising on his skin. "Wait—I've got some anesthetic spray."

"Don't." His hand closed on hers, and he was smiling. "It feels wonderful. Real."

"Oh, Christopher." Once again she was swept by that feeling of awe as she looked at him, of joy that was almost too much for her to contain. "It is real, isn't it? You're really here, alive...." Her hand tightened on his as her mind began to race from one incredible thought to another. "Do you realize the problems this creates? I mean, this has never happened before, there's not exactly a set of rules to follow.... You'll have to have a whole new identity, a job and papers and driver's license... not that that will be any trouble. My students do it all the time to buy beer and get into nightclubs. And God knows you can have any job you want. But none of that really matters does it?" A bubble of laughter came into her voice as she got to her knees, putting her coffee cup aside and looping her arms about his neck. "The only thing that matters is that you're here, even if I never understand how or what I did to deserve this...."

Christopher placed his own cup on the table, then turned back to her. His hand caressed her face, and his eyes were deep and rich with quiet certainty and joy. "Perhaps," he said, "we're not meant to understand.

Perhaps if there is one simple reason for all of this, it was that we could learn to accept the miracle without questioning. Sometimes there are no answers, Maggie. Sometimes there's simply love."

Maggie brought her forehead slowly to rest against his and closed her eyes. Tears burned behind her lids— tears of happiness, tears of gratitude, tears of wonder. And she thought if she spent a million years loving this man, it would not be long enough.

His hand caressed her back, fingering the material of her robe, and he said after a moment, "Do you know what else I'll need?"

Maggie smiled through the emotion that thickened her throat and said huskily, "What?"

"A marriage license."

She looked up at him.

"I've always said you needed to be married," he explained earnestly. "I would be honored if you would consider my proposal."

Maggie whispered, "There's no other proposal in the world I would ever consider."

He lowered her to the bed, her lips met his, and Maggie opened herself again to the joy that knew no bounds. He was here, he was real, and he was hers. Forever.

From *New York Times* Bestselling author
Penny Jordan, a compelling novel of ruthless passion
that will mesmerize readers everywhere!

Penny Jordan

Silver

Real power, true power came from
Rothwell. And Charles vowed to have it,
the earldom and all that went with it.

Silver vowed to destroy Charles, just as surely and
uncaringly as he had destroyed her father; just as he had
intended to destroy her. She needed him to want her . . .
to desire her . . . until he'd do anything to have her.

But first she needed a tutor: a man who wanted no one.
He would help her bait the trap.

**Played out on a glittering international stage,
Silver's story leads her from the luxurious comfort of
British aristocracy into the depths of adventure,
passion and danger.**

AVAILABLE IN OCTOBER!

 HARLEQUIN

Six exciting series for you every month... from Harlequin

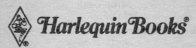

**From America's favorite author
coming in September**

JANET DAILEY

For Bitter Or Worse

Out of print since 1979!

Reaching Cord seemed impossible. Bitter, still confined to a wheelchair a year after the crash, he lashed out at everyone. Especially his wife.

"It would have been better if I hadn't been pulled from the plane wreck," he told her, and nothing Stacey did seemed to help.

Then Paula Hanson, a confident physiotherapist, arrived. She taunted Cord into helping himself, restoring his interest in living. Could she also make him and Stacey rediscover their early love?

Don't miss this collector's edition—last in a special three-book collection from Janet Dailey.
